DOCTOR WHO

Summer Falls

and Other Stories

BBC DOCTOR WHO

Summer Falls

and

Other Stories

BBC
BOOKS

1 3 5 7 9 10 8 6 4 2

Published in 2013 by BBC Books, an imprint of Ebury Publishing.
A Random House Group Company

Doctor Who is a BBC Wales production for BBC One.
Executive producers: Steven Moffat and Brian Minchin

The Random House Group Limited Reg. No. 954009

Addresses for companies within the Random House Group can be found at
www.randomhouse.co.uk

A CIP catalogue record for this book is available from the British Library.

ISBN: 978 1 849 90723 1

Commissioning editor: Albert DePetrillo
Series consultant: Justin Richards
Project editor: Steve Tribe
Production: Alex Goddard

Printed and bound in the USA

To buy books by your favourite authors and register for offers
visit www.randomhouse.co.uk

Contents

To My Daughter

Introduction

by Amelia Williams

It is simply delightful to be offered the chance to write an introduction to this collection. Gathered together here are three tales, huddling together for warmth under the covers. They all mean a great deal to me. One is, of course, my own *Summer Falls*, which introduced the world to the magical life of Kate Webster, 'The Girl Who Waited'. Another is *The Angel's Kiss* – the first book I read when I arrived in New York – and finally, the wonderful *The Devil In The Smoke* – a book which meant as much to me growing up as, I'm amazed to find, my own books have to some of their readers.

If you're wondering what connects these three tales, I have one word for you – ADVENTURE. Whether you're toting guns with Melody Malone, slaying nightmares with Madame Vastra, or even running across the ice with Kate Webster... these are all small worlds of adventure.

Before we go any further, though, I would like to thank a few people. My long-suffering husband, Rory (who is the very definition of tea and sympathy), my indefatigable editor Livia Silversteen and her pugs Lancelot and Guinevere who kept me sane during arduous afternoons arguing in her apartment. I would also like to thank my assistant Janette, who always knows where my glasses are and answers so many curious letters from my wonderful readers. And, of course there's also been help from the eagle eyes of Roderick Shellard, Paul Cantley, and the patient, nurturing advice from Barbara Balon, Robert Smith, Susan Gillingwater, Albert van Leopard, Nicola Payne, Terrance Unicorn and Frank Lee Madehamup.

Good. That was dull enough, I think. They've all stopped reading. Apart from **you**. It is just you, isn't it? I knew it would be. I knew that some day you'd find an old, jam-stained copy of this in a second-hand bookshop, brown pages smelling of caramel. I knew you'd pick it up and you'd smile that little smile (the one that does Fond while your eyes are doing Three Moves Ahead). You'd check the last page, and then you'd just wonder if there was anything else meant here for you, you lovely, silly raggedy man. Well, there is. But first, here's something important.

Whatever you do, keep your eyes on the page. On these words that you're reading right now. Don't stop reading. Because, your whole world may be about to change. Someone may be standing in front of you. No, Don't look up! Let me tell you what it is first. Because I know.

I keep seeing this figure. I keep seeing this old woman. Sometimes she'll be in a store. Sometimes she's at the far end of the block, weaving her way through the yellow cabs like she doesn't know the traffic's going the wrong way. I can tell when she's there – I get that prickling sensation that you do when you just know you're being watched. I'll turn around, and she'll be standing there, looking at me. She never talks to me. She just looks at me, and her smile is so sad. And then, oh, I don't know, a truck will go past, or a crowd of shoppers, and she'll be gone.

Rory and I – he's fine, thank you, teensy bit grey, but still my man – we went to Lake Erie last Fall. As every leaf fell it made things smell more autumny – that rich fragrance of old sap and smoky bonfires. There was a mist on the lake and SHE was there. The little old lady. She was standing at the end of the pier. Just looking at me, with that sad smile again. Rory was alarmed (his eyesight is still sharp as a pin). 'Is... she... standing... on... the... water?' Well, not quite. But nearly – she was waiting for me at the very end of the jetty, almost like she didn't want to be part of the world, and just vanish into the mist curling around her feet. (Get me. I are a writer.)

She was waiting for *me*. I knew that. She beckoned and I started towards her, but Rory's hand landed on my shoulder. 'Don't do this, Amy,' he said. 'Haven't you seen the films?'

'Which films?' I asked.

'Oh, I dunno, pretty much any film, really. Don't go talk to the creepy thing.'

'Yeah, well,' I said, 'It's not yet Halloween, we're

not planning on making out, and the guest house isn't built on an Indian pet cemetery.'

'Do you actually know that?' asked Rory.

'I'm frightened and I am blathering,' I told him tartly. 'I have so missed getting to do that.'

'Me too,' said Rory. 'Go talk to her.'

So I did.

'Hello,' she said, with a tiny wave. 'I probably shouldn't talk to you.'

'Who are you?'

She shrugged. 'I'm not sure it matters any more.'

'What does that mean?'

'Did you ever wonder if you were just living to do one thing?' Even for an odd old lady, she was odd.

'No!'

'Me neither,' she sighed, 'At least, not until it happened to me. Just one vivid Kodak moment and afterwards, life's all grey and normal and there's so much of it to get through.'

A coldness crept through me. Yes, I told her. I knew that feeling all too well.

I asked her what happened, but she wouldn't go into details. 'You might not believe it, anyhow.' She did the little laugh people do when something's not funny. 'It was all so long ago, and I was so young. But let's just say that there was a man. Quite unlike anyone else. And in among all the fire and madness and...' a pause '... stuff, I just knew I had to help him. It felt like what I was born for. Like I'd been waiting all my life just to grab hold of him and pull him out of the way of the lightning. And, afterwards, he just picked himself up, put out the flames on his coat, nodded to me and was away. Running.'

Oh.

She carried on. 'There was something about him. He was so shining and so familiar. Like I've done that before. Like I'll do it again.' She looked puzzled. 'But I've never seen anyone like him. Until I saw you. You've got that same glow to you – but it's fading now, isn't it?'

'Yes,' I said. I realised I was crying, which was quite surprising.

'So, I've been following you. In case… you need help.'

'No, sadly not,' I told her. 'Nothing big's exploded near me for quite some time. More's the pity.'

'Ah,' said the little old lady. 'Then, perhaps I can just ask you… if you knew him.'

I looked into her eyes. There was something dancing in them, like gold. 'Once,' I nodded. 'I had an imaginary friend. Only it turned out that he was real, and he never ever grew up.'

We both smiled at each other then. The same sad smile.

She spoke to me once more. 'Can you, I wonder, pass on a message for me?'

Now, this is the thing.

I knew that some day, you'd find an old, jam-stained copy of this in a second-hand bookshop, brown pages smelling of caramel. I knew you'd pick it up and you'd smile that little smile. That smile's frozen now. Because, for once, I'm the one that's

Three Moves Ahead. So, Doctor, get ready to look up. She is waiting for you. She's been waiting a long time. And if you do see a woman, just watching you, then that means that trouble's not far behind her.

But, just before you look up, I'll pass on her message:

'Run, you clever boy and remember...'

Summer Falls

Amelia Williams

1st Edition
1954

'When Summer Falls,
the Lord of Winter will arise...'

Chapter

1

It was the last week of the summer holidays, and Kate was in a temper. She banged around the kitchen until her mother told her to stop.

'Why, Kate, why?'

Kate sighed. She was sighing a lot latcly. 'Because, Mother, you are so untidy.'

Kate's mother glanced around the kitchen, and she knew her daughter was right. It was still full of packing cases, with half-washed dishes drying on cardboard boxes. 'I am not untidy!' she said hotly. 'I'm really going to get this sorted out. This morning. Probably. Now, it's a lovely day – why not go play down by the shore?'

'I would rather stay in and help you.' Kate did not like starting one thing before another was finished.

'Just… go off and have fun.' Her mother flicked her with the one tea towel that had so far come to light.

Kate stood outside the house. It was a pretty, old cottage with roses growing up to the thatched roof. It was all very nice, but it did not feel like home. The estate agent had explained that the old owner's possessions had not yet been cleared out. Kate's mother had vowed 'Don't worry, we'll soon have it shipshape,' and then done nothing about it.

Kate sighed. She made a resolution not to sigh any more. It was not getting her anywhere, and Kate did not believe in pointless activity.

She looked down the hill at the small town of Watchcombe, itself a jolly little monument to pointless activity. Twice a day a steam train deposited holidaymakers from the camp in the next bay, and they filled the winding streets, buying sweets and postcards and ordering teas. The beach was already scattered with families walking up and down in the sunshine, from the pontoon to the lighthouse and back – and, if they were speedy, doing it again for luck. Rowing boats set out from the small harbour – they went out a short way, did nothing much and came back. It all seemed quite pointless, and yet Kate could hear everyone calling happily to each other.

Kate could not see how they felt. 'Seven days,' she thought to herself glumly. A whole week until school started. New home, new town, new school. So much uncertainty. Kate was determined to Get

Something Done in the little time she had remaining. Seven days, although the bright morning was nearly gone already, so she would have to adjust it to six-and-a-half.

Kate thought about walking into town and perhaps catching the next train. She jingled the coins in her pocket and considered this as an option. True, Minehead had a better stationers, but buying a new rough book was simply admitting that, no matter how hard she tried to prevent it, School Was Going To Happen.

It was at this point that something unplanned occurred. It was the first in a series of unplanned events that would change Kate's life completely. A grey cat ran across the front lawn and paused, staring at her, about to vanish into the hedge.

Kate did not own a cat. She rather wanted one. As the cat appeared to be waiting for her, she made an exception to her rule of no unplanned activity, and followed it. It slipped nimbly through the hedge, and Kate pushed after it, with a little more difficulty than the cat, it is true. There was a moment when the branches crammed in around her and she wondered if she was stuck, and then she fell forwards, like a cork from a bottle, onto the grass. At the feet of a man.

'Hello,' he said. 'What brings you to my lawn?'

'Well,' Kate's mother had taught her to be unapologetic, 'your cat was trespassing in my garden. I am returning the favour.'

'That's a fair point,' admitted the man, helping

her up. 'Although it's not really my cat. Cats don't belong to anybody.'

Kate studied the man. He was tall, thin and friendly. She caught herself hoping he taught at her new school. If he did, she decided, she'd like school a bit more. 'I'm Kate Webster,' she said. 'How do you do?'

The man laughed and bowed. 'Then you are welcome to my grass, Kate Webster.' The cat weaved around their legs. The man bent down to scratch its ears. 'I say, Kate Webster,' he offered. 'Do your ears want scratching, too?'

Kate shook her head. 'Who are you?' she giggled.

To her surprise the man shrugged. 'Not anyone, really. I'm just looking after the museum for a friend. I guess you could call me the Curator. How does that sound?' He looked at her eagerly.

'Not very good,' admitted Kate. 'Don't you have a name?'

'I'm between names at the moment.' The man looked sheepish. 'I am having a holiday from them.'

'Can you do that?' asked Kate.

'I'm seeing how it works out,' admitted the Curator. 'Do you really think I need one? What do I look like? A Montmorency or a Keith?'

'How about Barnabas?' suggested Kate. It was the name of her teddy bear, and she thought more things should be called Barnabas.

'Barnabas!' The Curator seemed delighted. 'Never tried that one. Let's give it a whirl. Tea?'

He led her down the side of the house (which

seemed very nice, if a little boarded up) to the back, where some garden furniture was arranged around a large, striped canvas tent. The man vanished inside it, coming out with a tray heaped with cups, plates, scones and ginger pop. He rested it gently on the paving by the cat, which was cleaning itself.

'Why do you keep your kettle in your tent?' she asked.

'Oh, that's not a tent.' Barnabas had adopted the air of a man with a great secret. 'Inside there is my shed. It's undergoing repairs.'

That seemed an odd thing to say, but Kate's grandfather was very protective of his shed. Perhaps Barnabas was the same.

'I would give you the guided tour, but it's not finished,' he said, confirming her suspicions as he handed her a plate. 'Cheese scone. With sultanas in. I changed my mind halfway through.'

The cat looked at Barnabas wearily, and then sniffed the milk jug.

Tea went rather well. Barnabas listened to Kate's plan to Do Things before the end of the holiday and sagely suggested she draw up a timetable. He said that, if nothing else, it would take a while to do. 'Failing that,' he said, 'you could pop into my museum.' He caught the look on her face. 'It's really very nice. Though not on Wednesdays. I close it and spend the day going up and down on the steam train. I like trains.'

Kate wasn't entirely convinced.

'Don't you like it here?' The Curator sniffed.

'How odd. The 1950s aren't that bad, and this is a charming town. The kind of place you want to settle down and open a little shop with an e. I love a little shoppe. Have another scone.'

As Kate left Barnabas's house, the grey cat watched her go. It looked on the point of saying something, but then, like most cats, it never quite got around to it.

Kate stood in the lane, brushing crumbs from her pullover. The church clock struck noon. She was happy that she'd achieved something with her morning. A cool breeze swept in from the sea, reminding her that summer was nearly over. She walked down the lane, wondering if she could make friends with the boy next door before lunchtime. That'd really make something of the day.

It wasn't an unqualified success. The boy next door was sat outside the garage, mending a bike badly. He was quite handsome, but looked very sad. His misery increased when he caught Kate looking at him.

'Hello,' she said. 'You're Armand, aren't you?'

'Yes,' the boy scowled. 'But you probably shouldn't make friends with me, you know.'

'What?' Kate seemed genuinely puzzled. 'Is it because you're Indian?'

'No!' Armand laughed. 'They're all right about that. No...' He paused, sadly. 'It's because my father kills people.'

'Oh,' said Kate. She wondered what else to say. By the time she'd thought of something, a little too long had passed. Armand flushed, and went back to work. She stood there awkwardly, watching him mend his bike, and then went home for lunch.

Chapter

2

She waited until halfway through the tinned soup. 'Mum,' she asked, 'Does the man next door really kill people?'

Kate's mother gave her The Look. Clearly, there would be no help there.

Kate set herself an afternoon goal. She would find out what was going on, which sent her on a mission to Watchcombe. Armand's father worked at the pharmacy, so she decided on going there to buy soap or a fishing net. It was an old shop in the market square, its windows lined with yellow cellophane. Stood outside were two women, both giving the appearance of great bustle while standing still for a decent gossip. Kate lingered next to them, turning a critical eye to homes for sale in the window of the estate agent.

'Well,' tutted one to the other, 'I really shouldn't stop, as I must get some fishcakes for Arthur's tea.'

'Allerdyce is using more bread in 'em than he should,' said the other.

The first nodded. 'His batter's not fit neither,' and she thinned her lips. 'Not since his Lucy went away.'

'Oh this town,' the second clucked, and gave a significant glance at the pharmacy. 'Not what it was. Not what it was.'

'Old Miss Doyle is the latest. Natural causes, they said. But we know better, don't we?'

'Oh yes,' the first put in. 'No smoke without fire.' Satisfied, she turned away from the pharmacy and trotted down the street.

Kate went into the pharmacy, and rifled through a display of fishing nets and plastic spades. Next to this, an old dog slept in a basket. Behind the counter, a distinguished Indian man was handing a wrapped paper package to a severe-looking woman.

'Your prescription, madam.'

'Splendid. Thank you.' The woman made to put it in her shopping basket and then hesitated. 'I'm sure it's all in order, Mr Dass, but I was just wondering if Mr Stevens would mind checking?'

The paper bag hovered between them. Mr Dass's smile hung in place. 'It is precisely your prescription, Mrs Groves.'

She did not move. 'All the same...'

Mr Dass's smile lost its grip and fell from his face. With a startling suddenness, a twinkling old man burst from the back of the shop, heading off the explosion by plucking up the paper bag and opening it. 'We're only too happy, only too happy, Mrs Groves,' the little man laughed, holding the pill bottle up to the light. 'All in order. Don't take more than two, now, will you? We can't be too careful, can we?' He gave her the package, and this time it vanished into Mrs Groves's shopping basket.

With a cheerful 'Thank you, Mr Stevens,' she left the shop with a tinkle.

Mr Dass turned to his employer, his tone tight. 'I do wish you had let me handle it, sir. There was nothing wrong with the prescription.'

'Oh, absolutely not.' Mr Stevens beamed.

'There never has been anything wrong with any of my prescriptions. And...' Mr Dass's voice was rising. 'And I will not have it said... that there has been any mistake on my —'

Quick as smoke, Mr Stevens slid under the counter, and wrapped himself around Kate's shoulder. 'Now then, little girl, what have we here? You'd like to make some lovely sandcastles, wouldn't you?'

A minute later, Kate found herself standing outside the shop, holding a plastic bucket that had cost more than she'd wanted to pay, and for which she had no real use. Kate did not see the point of making something the sea would only wash away.

She went into a charity shop, and tried to give

them the bucket. 'Never used,' she insisted.

The jolly woman behind the counter was having none of it. 'That's one of Mr Stevens's, that is. We can't accept it. That,' and her tone was severe, 'would be taking trade away.'

Thwarted, Kate glanced around the shop. It was dingy, full of lace and candlesticks and incomplete jigsaws. In the corner was a cardboard box. The jolly woman's beady eyes saw Kate looking at the box. 'Ooh, that's from poor Miss Doyle's cottage, that is. Heaps of stuff to come from her place, my duck. Her nephew drove down just to turn his nose up at it, he did. "It's all junk," he told me, "and you're welcome to it." Terrible shame – she had a lot of local objets d'art. Your Mr Stevens, now he'd appreciate it. You have a look through, my dear, you'll find yourself a treasure. All in aid of the Orphans of Africa.'

Dutifully, Kate poked miserably through the box. It contained some small pottery owls glued to a pebble, a snow globe of the lighthouse, a jar of coloured sand... and a painting. At first she didn't like the picture at all. It showed the harbour, with dark seas crashing against the lighthouse. In the foreground were two odd figures. A man was holding a bright gold ring, and a woman had a large key. Kate was about to put it back among the paperweights and souvenirs when her fingers brushed against the surface of the painting. 'It's wet!' she gasped.

'Ah.' The jolly woman frowned. 'Miss Doyle's cottage did let in the damp something dreadful.

Mind,' she brightened, 'if it's in the walls, her nephew'll have a devil of a job letting it to holidaymakers.' Cheered by this bad news, she let Kate take the painting home at a discount, and consented, just this once, to taking Mr Stevens's bucket off her hands. For the orphans.

'Frightful!' exclaimed Kate's mother when she saw the painting. 'Take it to your room and clean it later.' She made Kate wash her hands twice before sitting her down to tea on a dining table cluttered with newspaper-wrapped plates. 'I've not made much progress,' sighed her mother. 'I just got so tired I had to have a nap.'

Kate's mother's life was ruled by naps. Good news, bad news, hard work or lack of work, all resulted in a little nap. Lately there had been a lot of bad news, and a considerable number of naps.

Kate pushed the corned beef spaghetti bolognese around her plate and told her mother all she had achieved. Mum brightened at the news that she'd made friends, but frowned slightly when she heard that she'd talked to Armand Dass. 'I mean,' she said, 'I'm not one to listen to gossip…'

Kate changed the subject to Barnabas, and her mother took a sudden dislike to her daughter having tea with strange men who lived in their sheds. 'He sounds peculiar company,' she muttered. 'But then again, a lot of people who look after museums are, I suppose. Never could stand the places. All about what's past and not what's to come. Still,' she considered, 'if it fills in a morning, perhaps you should pop in tomorrow.'

No expert in art restoration, her mother sent Kate up to clean the painting with a jam jar full of washing-up water and an old toothbrush. Kate covered the painting with suds and dabbed at it gingerly.

By the time she had finished, the water had gone from a light green to a thick black. The painting still felt wet – and her fingertips tingled. Almost like touching cotton wool.

When Kate slept that night, she dreamed she was somehow running across the sea, desperately trying to reach the lighthouse, but the waves heaved and towered around her. And something... something dark was following her.

Kate woke up, her heart pounding. She sat up in bed, gasping. Her room felt terribly cold and crammed full of menacing dark corners and nameless terrors hidden behind the neatly stacked crates. She was sharply aware that something was watching her... something... and her eyes fell on the window. Sat on the sill, gazing at her intently was Barnabas's grey cat. Despite herself, Kate giggled. The cat blinked and cleaned a paw.

'Well,' said Kate to herself, 'there's no going back to sleep after that. May as well make the most of the night.'

'Goodness,' said Kate's mother the next morning. 'The living room looks wonderful. Clearly I managed a lot more unpacking than I thought yesterday.'

Kate stifled a yawn. 'I'll make you some breakfast.'

'Oh, would you?' Kate's mum sank into an armchair and drew her dressing gown around her. 'You're an angel! I always make such a mess of the frying pan.'

Kate found the cat in the lane. She greeted it politely. It stared at her, and seemed about to respond when a stone flew past its ear. The cat reared up and darted into a bush.

Kate turned around. Armand was standing there.

'What did you do that for?' she asked.

'Can't stand cats,' he said. He laughed, but there was something sheepish about him. Would quite like to be a bully, but was too much of a coward, Kate decided. 'You shouldn't be cruel,' she said. 'I've got something to show you.' She pulled the painting out of her satchel and showed it to him proudly.

Armand looked unimpressed. He ran a finger along it and shivered. 'What's it painted on? It feels weird. Is that mould? Throw it away.'

Kate had been hoping for a better response. She packed it back in her bag. 'Are you still mending that bicycle?'

Now Armand masked his sheepishness with anger. 'You wouldn't understand,' he snapped. 'The chain's all sticky.'

'Yes,' sighed Kate, seating herself on the concrete in front of the corpse of the bicycle. She spun a wheel and considered it. 'The problem is that you've been greasing the chain with cooking oil. Fetch me a bucket of hot soapy water and let's see what we can do.'

Some time later, Armand had got used to watching her work. 'Have you always been like this?' he asked.

Kate considered the question and decided it was silly. 'It's like me asking if you've always been like you are.'

'I don't understand.'

'Well, I think you're actually nice. But you go to a lot of trouble not to be. Has that always been the case?'

Armand thought for a moment, then playfully splashed her with suds.

'That proves my point,' laughed Kate. 'You're trying to avoid answering. Is it because of the gossip about your father?'

Armand didn't try to hide his anger this time. 'You wouldn't understand,' he growled. 'Anyway, you haven't got any friends.'

'I haven't,' agreed Kate. 'But as I've only just moved to this town it would be unreasonable to expect me to have any. But I am sure I shall make some.'

'How?' asked Armand.

'By mending bicycles,' said Kate.

'This is quite a remarkable painting,' said Barnabas.

He had been working in his tent rather than in his museum. Kate found this odd, but was relieved to have been spared the walk.

'Can you tell me anything about it?' she asked.

Barnabas swept back his tangled hair and peered closely at the painting. He sniffed it curiously. 'You've cleaned it with washing-up liquid. And had cabbage for lunch,' he announced. 'Funny sort of canvas. Almost like tin foil.'

Kate nodded.

'Interesting. But ooh, feels like static electricity, doesn't it?'

Kate nodded again.

'If,' sighed Barnabas, 'static was a bit damp.'

They stared at the painting for a bit.

'I don't like it,' admitted Barnabas. 'It's by Mitchell. He was a local painter a long time ago. Supposed to have gone a bit loopy in the end. Curious.' He regarded it again solemnly.

'I think it's a puzzle,' said Kate.

'Oh?'

'Well, if you don't look at the sea and the sky, but just at the painting. At the top is the lighthouse. The man's holding a ring, the woman a key. They form a triangle. Perhaps it tells you how to find the objects.'

'I suppose it might.' Barnabas ran a thumb along the frame. 'Is this the title?'

Kate nodded. 'I tried cleaning it with an old toothbrush but can't make it out.'

'A toothbrush, eh?' Barnabas clucked disapprovingly and angled the frame to catch the light. Then his smile stopped and he looked solemn. 'It's called *The Lord of Winter*.'

'What does that mean?' asked Kate.

'I don't know.' Clearly the Curator did. 'Why don't we pop down to the museum and look at this properly? Before doing anything. Like, perhaps, trying to solve the puzzle. Do nothing, yes? I say – you haven't shown anyone else this have you?'

'No,' said Kate. 'Only a friend.'

'Oh well, that's all right then,' said Barnabas. He was suddenly all serious and old. 'It's just... I don't think that painting's very nice.'

The doorbell rang.

'Can you get that, Kate?' her mother called down. 'I am having a nap.'

Kate ran to the door and opened it.

Standing there was Armand's father, Mr Dass.

'Hello,' she said.

Mr Dass muttered something.

'Would you like a cup of tea?' she asked.

Mr Dass's eyes darted about nervously.

Kate took him into the kitchen and put the kettle on the hob. 'I am sorry about the mess,' she said. She decided to use the time it would take the water to boil to learn new information. 'We are still unpacking. And there are so many of Mrs Mitchell's old things lying around.'

Mr Dass muttered again.

'What was she like?' Kate prodded while she located mugs.

Mr Dass stared at her.

'She was your neighbour. Was she nice?'

Mr Dass eventually managed a whispered 'Yes.'

'Oh, I am pleased,' said Kate, pouring milk into cups. 'I don't like to think of living somewhere someone unpleasant lived. I have her bedroom. It's full of her books. There's even some of her clothes in the wardrobe. Mum says we'll clear it all out soon, but I daresay we won't get around to it. We never really do. We should have done it before we starting unpacking, but we haven't, so it probably won't happen. Sugar?'

Mr Dass nodded. Kate worried that she was talking too much. She picked up her tea. It was too hot to actually drink, so she just pretended to sip it. She decided that if she made a little slurp it was quite convincing.

Mr Dass spoke. 'I would like to buy your painting,' he said.

Kate put her tea down. 'Oh,' she said.

'I will pay twice what you did for it,' he said.

'The painting is not for sale,' Kate was firm. 'And, your son owes me an apology. I told Armand as a secret. How disappointing that he told you.'

'That's not important.' Mr Dass waved a hand, and strode towards her. 'I really must have that painting.' He was standing quite close to her and breathing very hard.

Frightened, Kate wondered about running, but she was backed into a corner. 'I do think I should ask my mother's permission before making a decision,' she said carefully, before calling 'Mum!' very loudly.

But Kate's mother showed no signs of coming.

Mr Dass smiled. It wasn't a nice smile. 'I think,' he said, 'you will fetch me the painting now.'

'No,' said Kate.

'Give me that painting.'

Mr Dass's hand clamped around her wrist.

Kate was about to shout for help when something grey streaked through the kitchen window at Mr Dass.

He reeled back, clutching at his cheek. The grey cat ran across the draining board, knocking over a mug.

Kate's mother appeared, rubbing sleep out of her eyes. 'You woke me up,' she yawned. 'And look at the mess you've made. Oh, hello.' She acknowledged Mr Dass with surprise.

'Your cat attacked me,' Mr Dass murmured.

'Oh no,' Kate's mother shook her head. 'We don't have a cat.' She paused. 'Do we?'

Kate, busy with a dustpan and brush, shook her head.

'Well, there we are then. So nice to have met you. That's quite a nasty scratch you've got. You should put a plaster on it right away. I would do it, but I've no idea where ours are.' Kate's mother swept Mr Dass out of the house and pottered back into the kitchen.

'Do we like him?' she asked. 'I don't think we do.'

Kate emptied the dustpan into the bin and hugged her mother. 'Thank you, mum. I do love you.'

'I see.' Kate's mother patted her head and yawned again. 'I was having such a strange dream. It was very cold and dark and...' Her eyes alighted on Kate's mug. 'Oh, you've made me a cup of tea,' she smiled. 'How thoughtful.'

That night, Kate dreamed again about the painting. She'd propped it up on the dressing table. It seemed oddly at home, surrounded by all Mrs Mitchell's dusty objects and old trinkets. Kate drifted off to sleep wondering who Mrs Mitchell was, and imagining what she was like. Kate was just deciding that, overall, Mrs Mitchell was a kindly woman, if a bit serious, when she slept, and the dreams of the painting came.

She was running up the steps round the outside of the lighthouse. They were frozen with ice and it was so cold. The steps wound up and around, up and around, but they didn't seem to end. And there was a noise – over the roaring of the sea and someone calling her name, there was a scratch, scratch, scratching...

Kate woke up. There was a scratching in her room. At first she thought of mice. Kate did not like mice. She flicked on the bedside lamp and dared herself to look at the source of the scratching. It sounded quite large, and she hoped it was not a rat. A mouse would be better than a rat, although still very hard to deal with. Perhaps she could just hide under the covers and hope that it would go away and...

Kate peeped. It was not a rat. Or a mouse. It was the Curator's grey cat. It was scratching at the floorboards and glancing at her. As though she should help.

Kate slipped out of bed. Her room was freezing. She crouched down next to the cat.

'What is it?' she asked.

The cat did not answer.

'How did you get in here?'

The cat did not answer that either.

'You want me to lift this floorboard, don't you?'

The cat seemed to nod.

Hoping that there wasn't a nest of mice under the floorboards, Kate tugged at it. It lifted.

Under the floorboard, snuggled under mounds of dust and old wiring, was a dirty old metal ring. Kate lifted it up and caught it in the moonlight.

It was the ring from the painting.

Kate's mother had said that she was only to be woken in emergencies. She had previously defined an emergency as the house being on fire, and not Kate discovering an interesting new word or even inventing a new colour.

Kate wondered if the present situation qualified as an emergency. She now owned a strange painting, one wanted by a man who may have been poisoning people. Kate wondered if Mr Dass had killed Mrs Mitchell. If so, was it because he wanted the ring she had found hidden under the floorboard? She remembered the Curator's warning not to try and find the objects in the painting. But she hadn't. It was all the cat's doing. Mostly.

Kate had poked around the space between the joists again and discovered an old envelope. Written on it in a jumpy hand were the words 'Keep it safe. He must not find what the Cold Lady holds.' Was this the ring? And was the 'he' Mr Dass? Was the Cold Lady the woman from the painting? So many important questions.

But, on balance, these things had remained hidden for a long time so perhaps this wasn't an actual emergency. Undecided, Kate stood outside her mother's door and called her name a couple of times at a normal volume. If it really was an emergency, then fate would make sure that her mother woke up.

Her mother did not wake up, so Kate decided to go back to sleep. I'll sort it out in the morning, she thought. At the foot of the bed was the painting, the ring lying on top of it, and the grey cat curled up, as if guarding them all. Kate slipped between the covers, feeling the cat warm against her legs. She slept.

Chapter

3

When Kate woke up, it was winter.

She didn't notice for a while. First she spotted the cat had gone. Then she realised how cold it was. She could see her breath fogging in the bedroom air. She got out of bed, startled at the icy chill of the floorboards beneath her feet. A hurried search for slippers was fruitless, and she raided Mrs Mitchell's wardrobe for a very old-fashioned winter coat that reeked of mothballs. She put on three pairs of mismatched socks and stomped downstairs.

Now above all, she'd like her mother to have made her a cup of tea. But there was no sign of her. Not in the kitchen, her napping chair, or even in bed. Perhaps she'd gone out. Kate peered out of a window.

It was at this point that Kate realised that it had snowed. She looked at the snow. 'That's beautiful,' she breathed. 'But quite ridiculous. It's September the third.'

Despite her saying this, the snow stayed where it was. Inches of thick, proper, glorious snow, all the way down the garden, the road and into town.

'Interesting,' said Kate. 'No footprints. So either Mum went out before the snow or...'

But Kate couldn't work out what 'or...' would be. So she made herself a cup of tea and then went on the hunt for Wellington boots and gloves.

Kate crumped through the snow. It was all hers. All her life, she had wanted to be the first person to walk in the snow, but she had never managed it. No matter how early she woke up, someone had always got there first. But not now.

It may have been the last week of summer but already Kate had made two friends, found a painting and a ring, mended a bicycle, and been the first person to walk in the snow.

Kate rang Barnabas's doorbell. He wasn't in. She passed Armand's house. It seemed empty. She did not want to ring the doorbell as she did not feel in the mood to talk to either Armand or his father.

She walked down the road to find someone in the town. But all the streets she walked through were deserted. The houses were dark, the cars buried under snow. Even though it was daytime, the streetlights glowed faintly.

It was silent. Utterly silent. Which was when Kate realised what was wrong. The sound that was missing. She ran down to the harbour and stared.

The sea was frozen.

Kate stood, watching the sea for a long time. She'd never seen anything so impossible, so beautiful. She looked out at the waves frozen into mountain peaks, stretching towards a distant, dark sky, and she felt afraid. She was alone in a world that was a dream.

She thought she heard something. A distant shout, perhaps, echoing off the wall of water. She called out to it, but there was no reply. And then she noticed something.

There were prints in the snow. Tiny prints. Paw prints. She ran after them, her boots sinking deep into the snow, going past the tiny sailing boats stuck to the sea, past a row of cafés and an old inn… to the harbour wall. Sat on the wall, looking out to sea, ears perked up, was the grey cat.

It turned to look at her, unblinking. Kate had never been so glad to see anything in her life, and made to sweep it up. But it edged back.

'Oh, cat,' said Kate. 'This is just impossible. I was upstairs. Asleep. Then this happened. It doesn't make any sense. How can this have happened? Did someone do this?'

'I did,' the cat replied, much to her surprise.

That stumped Kate for a moment. Eventually, she said, 'I have two questions.'

'Go on.'

'How can I speak cat?'

The cat yawned, considering. 'It would be better to say that I can speak human. Next.'

'And are you sure you did this?'

The cat nodded. 'Oh yes. I suggested you bring together the painting and the ring.'

'But why?'

'I wanted to make sure you did it.' The cat shrugged a paw. 'I wanted to see what would happen.'

'What? Why would you do such a thing?'

'I am, after all, a cat.' The cat nibbled at its claws thoughtfully. 'I work for no one. I was just curious.' It worried away at a tough bit of fur. 'And I do rather want to meet the Lord of Winter.'

'Who?' Kate felt very much out of her depth.

The cat looked up, witheringly. 'You are a slow purr. That's what's written on the frame of the painting. "When Summer Falls, The Lord Of Winter Will Arise."'

'But...' Kate was annoyed – the cat had not answered her question, which was hardly playing fair. 'Who is the Lord of Winter?'

The cat emitted a short yowl of exasperation. 'I'm not going to tell you everything, young kitten.' And, with a shake of its tail, it vanished over the harbour wall.

Kate ran forward with a gasp – but the creature hadn't drowned. She could see it, darting between the icy foothills of the frozen sea, tail up, hunting.

*

As the snow fell, the town became more beautiful, still and silent. And yet Kate caught a sob starting at the back of her throat. Kate rarely cried. She plunged her hands into the snow on the harbour wall, feeling the chill spread into her bones. For almost the first time in her life, she had no idea what to do. Instead of coming out in their usual neat order, her thoughts were tumbling. She kept her hands pushed into the snow until her brain slowed down, until its one thought was 'please can you take your hands out of the snow?'

Kate did and immediately felt a little better. She was alone. All the grown-ups had gone. The only thing alive was a talking cat. And someone was coming, this mysterious Lord of Winter. The sky seemed darker now than ever. Perhaps it was nearly night time. Did that make sense? When had she woken up? Kate walked to the lighthouse at the end of the harbour. Remembering her dreams, she reached for the gate to the metal steps. Normally the gate was padlocked and a polite notice asked people to keep out and not to fish from the pier. Both padlock and notice were gone.

This was an invitation either to open the gate or go fishing. Kate did not like fishing. The gate swung open with a creak, and she started up the metal steps. They wound up the building in a spiral, and she soon found herself breathless. As her heart started to thump in her chest she remembered her dreams. The steps had gone on endlessly, and something had been following her. She made herself stop and look back. Nothing was following her. And yet she felt as though the sky was watching her.

With a push, Kate made it to the top of the lighthouse, bursting out breathless onto the roof. The platform around the light was icy and she skidded into the rail, flailing against it. She had a moment of panic and terror, gazing into the sea below, and then dizzily sank down onto the platform, grabbing the railing.

This would not do. She stood up and faced the sea. It took her a while before she admitted that actually, she was just crouching, gripping the railing with both hands, but she was still trying. Up here, the silence wasn't so absolute – a cold wind tugged at her hair, and she could just hear a distant cracking and splintering, as if of breaking glass. This puzzled her for a minute, until she discerned that the frozen sea was not totally solid, its sudden hills shifting and bumping against each other.

She peered into the horizon beyond the sea. The bleached grey of the sunless sky was shadowed – was it a cloud drifting closer, or a ship or something else? She squinted, but couldn't quite see. Yet, in the distance, something dark was approaching.

Kate shivered, and not entirely with cold. She stood watching for a while, attempting to discern what it was, or how fast it was travelling. She couldn't tell – and yet, she did notice something else.

Kate heard the crying. It wasn't an animal or a bird – it was the sound of someone down below feeling thoroughly sorry for themself. Well, she thought, there's someone other than me in town and they need cheering up. That's something.

She picked her way carefully down to the harbour. The sound was fainter on the ground, but she knew roughly which direction it came from. She clumped past the town's sad-looking Chinese restaurant, and down an alley. She found a set of footsteps and followed them. The crying grew louder.

She found Armand by the bins, slumped against an old shopping basket. He was shaking with tears.

'Oh hello,' she said, trying to sound casual. 'Fancy seeing you here.'

Armand looked miserable She'd originally thought him older than her, but not now. He was no longer angry, arrogant, or distant – just thoroughly wretched. He blinked at her, but did not stop crying.

'Right then,' said Kate, and slipped off her coat. 'You're coming with me.'

Chapter

4

Gino's was the town's grandest café. It disdained day-trippers seeking cooked breakfasts and sliced ham. It preferred to serve creaking pensioners cheese scones and gossip. On any given day it was full of customers happily complaining to waitresses about old scores and tired bones. But now it was empty.

The door swung ajar. A slice of snow had pushed its way in. Kate swept it out before shutting the door firmly. She sat Armand down at a table with an artificial daffodil. She handed him a creased magazine, then went out to the kitchen to do battle with the gas stove. A couple of minutes later she brought them out two mugs of soup and some not-too-stale bread.

For a few moments, the two sat, sipping and

staring at each other.

'Hmm,' said Kate.

Armand blew on his soup. 'Did you cause all this?' he demanded.

Kate was startled. 'Uh, no,' she said. 'I thought it was something to do with you. I mean, why else would you be here?'

'That's what I was thinking about you,' Armand retorted. He found some pepper, cascading it over his soup.

'How can you drink it like that?' laughed Kate.

'It's nice,' Armand replied. 'So you didn't do this?'

'A cat has claimed responsibility,' she said airily. 'Which is ridiculous. But you know the cat that belongs to the museum curator? It's here. And... it spoke to me... or, at least, I think it did and...' She trailed off. 'Pass the pepper, would you?'

Armand slid the pepper pot across the table.

They carried on drinking soup. Outside more snow fell.

'I suppose we're stuck here,' said Armand. 'I've tried calling the police, but the phones are dead.'

'They would be.' Kate finished the last piece of bread. 'We could try walking to the main road. But I think we're trapped here. Something's wrong with the world.'

'Did the cat tell you what's going on?' asked Armand.

'A bit.' Kate explained about the painting and the ring that the cat had found.

'I'm wondering if we're here because...' she thought about it, 'we both touched the painting.'

'So that third object – somewhere out there is a woman with a key?'

'I think so,' said Kate. 'We should start looking. Once you've finished your soup.'

Which is how they found Milo. He was a small, blond child wearing only a pair of swimming trunks. He was sobbing loudly.

'What is it about the boys in this place?' Kate allowed herself a sigh. 'Do they spend all their time crying?'

'If he didn't blub so loudly, we wouldn't have found him,' pointed out Armand.

'True,' admitted Kate.

Milo was curled up on the veranda of the bowling club. Cradled in his arms was a small, unhappy-looking dog.

'I don't like dogs,' announced Kate.

'Cat person,' explained Armand.

'Ah,' Milo sniffed. His tears dripped onto his dog's fur. The dog licked at them, a puzzled expression on his face.

Kate had heard that dogs were like their owners. Milo's dog looked loyal, but confused by the world.

'We were bathing on the beach,' Milo said. 'With Mum and Auntie Jean. We came from the holiday camp for the day. I drifted off to sleep in the sunlight with Brewster in my arms... and when I woke up... I was all alone, and it was cold and my towel was frozen and Mum is going to be very, very cross when she finds me…' He considered his options. 'So I ran away. But I want to go home. I want my mummy.'

'Well—' began Kate, but Milo forestalled further conversation with a bout of crying that showed no signs of stopping.

'Fine.' Kate broke into the bowling clubhouse. She emerged a few minutes later with an old jumper that smelled of spilt beer. 'Put this on,' she said, 'otherwise you'll freeze.'

She handed round some odd gloves she'd found in lost property. 'There,' she said. 'Now we're ready to go investigating.'

'We are?' Milo stared at her with saucer-eyes. 'But when are the grown-ups coming? Aren't we going to find some adults?'

'Was I this bad?' Armand asked her. Kate ignored him.

'No,' she informed Milo firmly. 'We are on our own. There are no grown-ups here. Our only chance is to sort this out ourselves. Now, give me the key.'

Milo stared at her in confusion and alarm. And then burst out crying again.

Armand looked at her and smirked.

'Right then.' Kate banged a mug of soup down on the café table. Milo seized it gratefully and his sobs subsided. 'This café is our Headquarters. We have a puzzle to solve and a key to find. Are you quite sure you haven't got it?'

Milo shook his head, his teeth chattering. At his

feet, Brewster lapped gratefully at a bowl of water. The dog seemed to be handling events rather well. Kate crouched down and stared into the dog's eyes. 'What's going on, Brewster?' she asked him. 'It's all right. You can tell me.'

The dog stared back at her, growled, and went on with drinking water.

'What are you doing?' Milo asked slowly.

'She thinks she can talk to animals,' Armand sneered.

'That's not true!' Kate stood up with as much dignity as she could. 'It was just the one cat that could talk.'

'Can we go and find your cat?' suggested Milo. 'Brewster's good with cats. He's had some topper scraps with them.'

'I'm sure he has,' said Kate, 'But it may not be the best way to interrogate the cat. It seemed to have told me all it wanted to. It said that the painting was important.'

'Can I see it?' asked Milo. 'I'd be only too happy to.'

'I don't have it on me,' admitted Kate. How annoying. If only, she thought to herself, she had some kind of device that would fit in her pocket and take pictures and show them on a screen. Perhaps, she thought, she'd get around to inventing one. When she grew up. 'I'm afraid it's back at the house.'

'Along with the ring?' asked Armand. 'Isn't that a bit silly?'

'I'd not really thought about that,' agreed Kate.

'I mean, we're fine so long as we're the only people here.'

'I would like to see the painting,' said Milo. 'It sounds wizard.'

'Fine,' said Kate. 'I'll nip home and get it. Don't go anywhere. And leave me a little soup.'

Kate hurried across the harbour, snow biting into her face. The sky hovered just overhead, pressing down. She thought she could touch the clouds if she stood on tiptoe. Out across the sea, the darkness was spreading, the shadow getting closer. She could swear that there was less sea now – as though the world was closing in around them.

The wind whipped up, and Kate grasped the wall to steady herself. She'd hoped to be there and back in five minutes, but this was proving to be a struggle.

From nowhere, the cat leapt onto the wall, staring into her face, curious. Then it smiled.

'Hello, Kate,' it said. 'Things aren't going too well.'

'Tell me about it. This is your fault.'

'But I'm cold,' the cat complained.

'Well then, you shouldn't have caused all this.'

'I'm a cat,' it sighed. '*Je ne regrette rien*. Now, feed me and warm me up.'

So Kate picked the cat up and got ready to carry it home. It vanished inside her duffle coat and purred loudly.

'Oh.' Its head poked out. 'There's something you should know. Look down at the jetty.'

Kate looked down at the snow-covered decking. There were footsteps on it. They were not alone.

The house felt strange, ticking and creaking, chuckling at Kate. A window banged in the kitchen, startling her.

'Is someone in here?' Kate called out.

No answer.

'Mum?'

No answer.

Kate looked at the cat. 'What's going on? Is someone here?'

'They were,' the cat sniffed the air, 'But they left a few minutes ago. I don't think they found what they wanted.'

'How can you tell?'

The cat trotted to the front door. 'They came in this way. They smelled excited.' It shook a paw at the kitchen. 'They went out that way – and they smelled angry.'

'Ah. Were they looking for the painting?'

'Of course.' The cat found a bit of carpet and cleaned itself. 'But I hid it. You reek of dog, by the way. You should change your coat.'

'You hid the painting?' Kate exclaimed. 'Where?'

The cat paused. 'Stop asking me questions. When you interrupt, I have to start cleaning all over from the beginning.'

'No you don't, that's silly.'

The cat looked at her pityingly. 'Those are the rules of cleaning.' It stuck its tongue out at her then went back to licking a paw.

'So where's the painting?'

Exasperated, the cat stood and trotted upstairs. 'Fine, fine, I'll show you. Then I'm going to clean myself thoroughly on this chair by the radiator.'

The cat led her to her bed and vanished under the covers.

Kate waited.

And waited.

Eventually she prodded the cat-shaped lump.

'Ow,' said the cat. 'What?'

'Where's the painting?'

'Ooops,' admitted the cat. 'Sorry. Totally forgot about that. Just having a little shuteye. It's warm and dark in here. I'm sitting on your painting.'

Thinking how well the cat would get on with her mother, Kate drew back the covers. The cat was curled up on the painting and the ring. She picked them up.

'Right then. I've got a world to save.'

She ran away.

'Whatever,' said the cat, watching her go until its eyelids became heavy and it went back to sleep.

The café was deserted. This was typical of boys. They never listened to girls and got bored easily. She could not understand it. There was, after all, plenty of soup left. Admittedly, it was minestrone, but still. Crossly, she realised the boys had not washed their mugs. Hiding the painting and the ring under a table, she washed up, and then set out.

It was getting colder. As she traipsed through the empty streets, the snow became heavier, pressing into her face. Every house front, every car was now buried. The only colour was the red of her gloves. Everything else was white. White apart from that dark stain spreading across the horizon, coming closer across the creaking mountains of the frozen sea.

Something fluttered in her stomach. Kate realised she was afraid.

Which was when she heard the phone ringing.

The trill echoed up and down the streets, drawing her closer and closer to a small building in the harbour. Kate stopped outside the door, rubbing her sleeve across the brass plate, clearing it of snow: 'Watchcombe Museum.' She pushed through, her boots thunderously loud on the boards after all that quiet snow.

She took three steps and gasped. The museum looked like someone had stuffed a bookshop into a junkshop into a boat into a church. Brass musical instruments hung from fishing nets looped through the rafters. Display cases shone with books and maps, stretching away into the furthest corners of the lobby and beyond. It was very impressive.

But what had made Kate stop were the wet boot prints ahead of her. They headed across the lobby, past a large waxwork of Queen Victoria and into a room full of stuffed bears and an Ormolu clock. Kate swallowed and entered the room.

'Hello?' she called.

There was no answer, but the glass eyes of the bears stared at her. The phone continued to ring. She looked around, trying to see if anyone was watching her. Above her, a whale skull bit the air in two. The bell rang on. She ran through to the next room, which appeared to be mostly jigsaws. Still no sign of the telephone.

'Answer it!' she yelled. She knew she wasn't alone. They may as well do something useful.

The next room contained a painting of the Battle of Waterloo and a reproduction of Drake's cabin on the *Golden Hind*. Incongruously sat on the desk among the scrolls was a brass telephone.

She reached out for it.

The telephone stopped ringing.

Kate looked around herself and then kicked the desk firmly.

'Right then,' she called out at the top of her voice, 'I know you're in here. I know I'm not alone. Instead of being creepy you could have picked up, you know. It wouldn't have hurt you. That was the real world, trying to help us.'

Nothing.

She called out again, louder. 'Can you hear me? My name is Kate Webster and I am going to find you. And when I do, I am not going to be scared. I am going to be very cross indeed.'

Something moved in the next room. It was a small ball, rolling across the floorboards. She picked it up. It was wet.

'Right,' Kate threw it, and, as she'd expected,

Brewster came bounding out from behind a desk, and brought it to her.

'Milo,' she said. 'I have your dog. Come out now. Otherwise… I dunno.' She glanced at Brewster, who looked back at her with adoration. 'I guess I'll end up making dog soup. Is that a thing?'

Sheepishly, Milo emerged from hiding, bringing a scowling Armand with him.

'We thought,' admitted Armand, 'that it was someone else. Someone bad. We didn't realise it was you. Then you started shouting at us—'

'And then we *really* hoped it was someone else,' finished Milo.

Kate glared at them.

'That phone call could have been important,' she seethed. 'Could you really not bring yourselves to answer it, whatever the risk?'

Each boy hoped the other would say something.

'I guess we were scared,' muttered Armand.

Milo, gratefully, nodded. 'And not thinking straight.'

'Right,' said Kate, and allowed herself a sigh. She really had a very low opinion of boys. And then a suspicious thought tugged at her. 'Did one of you stop the other from answering the phone?' she asked before she could stop herself.

The two glanced at each other guiltily.

'No.' Armand was quick.

'I see.' Kate knew it – she knew she was right not to trust Armand. The boy was definitely up to something. 'Why did you come here?' she asked.

'It was my idea.' Milo was proud. 'I thought that, if we were trying to find this key, we should look for it in the museum. Museums are very useful places,' he finished.

Kate had always considered museums to be a little dull. She liked this one, although she would have enjoyed spending a week putting it in a really good order.

'And did you find anything?' she asked.

'I think so,' said Milo. 'We found an exhibition on the painter. He's really very clever.'

The boys led her to a little annex that smelt of damp. Hung in it were several works by local artists, including several by the same hand. All were various views of the town in winter, and all were signed 'Mitchell'. There was a small leaflet and a donation box. Kate, lacking any money, popped an old badge in there as an IOU.

Armand picked up a copy of the leaflet without even glancing at the donation box, and read aloud. 'The last in a long line of Mitchells to have lived in Watchcombe, Mitchell painted a considerable number of scenes of local beauty before going away to serve in the Great War. He did not return.'

'How sad,' said Kate.

'They're jolly good, aren't they?' enthused Milo.

'They look just like your painting, don't they?' said Armand.

'Disappointingly.' Truth to tell, Kate was starting to think of the mysterious Mr Mitchell as a bit of a one-trick pony. He liked painting sea, sunsets and snow. Over and over again…

'Well, I rather like them,' Milo said, crossly.

'I'm sure they're very nice if you like that sort of thing, but they're all so alike,' Kate mused.

'So what,' asked Armand triumphantly, 'Makes the painting you've got so special?'

'Good point.' Kate blinked.

This started a whole new train of thought which crashed to a halt when the telephone rang again.

Chapter

5

Kate rushed to the room, pursued by the boys, and grabbed the receiver.

'Hello? Hello? Hello!' she gabbled.

'Goodness, you sound like you're having fun!' came the voice at the other end.

'Barnabas!' she gasped. 'What are you doing?'

'Hoping someone would pick up the phone,' came the answer. 'Hello, Kate Webster, I'm glad it's you.'

'Where are you?'

There was a short pause. 'I'm out of town,' he said. 'And, to be strictly honest, having more than a little trouble getting back in. But don't worry. Help is on the way.'

'You've called the police? The fire brigade? The coastguard?'

'No,' Barnabas admitted. 'I'm help. I'm on the way.'

'The town's frozen, all the people are gone, and something bad's happening. You're just a museum curator. How can you help?'

'Take a deep breath.'

'What?'

'It will calm you down.'

Kate took a deep breath.

'Now,' said Barnabas's voice, sounding a long way away. 'Here's how I can help. What's happening to the town has something to do with its past. And museums are all about the past. Which is where I come in. Hopefully. If I can get there in time.'

'But—' shouted Kate.

'Deep breath!' admonished Barnabas.

'Deep breaths just allow me to shout louder,' Kate informed him. 'It's all very well to know that you're on your way, but please also call on a responsible adult.'

'You don't need a responsible adult. You need me. Listen—'

Kate realised she was the only grown-up in the world.

She hung up.

'What did you do that for?' gasped Armand.

'He was being silly.'

'Who was that?' demanded Milo.

'It was the museum curator.'

'Who's that?' asked Milo.

'My neighbour. This is his museum. He says he's

coming to help.'

'Well, he won't be able to.' Milo looked serious. Tears were not far off. 'We're trapped here and we're going to die.'

Kate braced herself to be comforting and the phone rang again.

This time Armand picked it up.

'It's for you.' He offered her the receiver.

'I know,' said Kate.

'He's really very insistent.'

'He'd better be.'

She took the telephone.

'You hung up on me.'

'I know.'

'But why?'

'It's a very interesting museum,' said Kate. 'And you weren't being very helpful.'

'I see.'

There was a pause.

'Right then. Your painting shows two objects. It's like a treasure map. You just have to find the objects.'

'Worked that out. Got the ring already.'

'You did? I told you not to.'

'I know. Your cat found the ring.'

'Oh. Grey cat, funny whiskers, doesn't laugh at jokes?'

'That's the one.'

'Hmm. No tuna for him.'

'And now we're trying to find the other one. The key held by the lady.'

'The Cold Lady,' mused Barnabas.

'What?'

'I was about to tell you.' Barnabas sounded annoyed. 'Somewhere in my museum is an old poem –

When Summer Falls,
The Lord of Winter will arise
When darkness calls
And opens the Cold Lady's eyes.'

'Who is the Lord of Winter, anyway?'

'Trouble. It's why I've got to get there. And believe me, I'm trying.' Over the phone came a small explosion and terrible grinding noise. Kate assumed this was Barnabas's car.

'You should be more careful changing gears,' she informed him.

'Thank you.' Barnabas spoke through gritted teeth. 'You're proving quite hard to get to.'

'We're all alone. It's just the three of us.'

'We?'

'Me, Armand, and a young boy called Milo, Oh, and his dog. Hurry. We're running out of soup.'

There was another grinding of gears. Over this Kate heard the Curator tell her to ask his cat about the Lord of Winter and to be very careful about who she decided to trust.

Mind you, she thought, Barnabas must have been calling her from his car. This seemed an odd thing to her. Even in London there weren't telephones in motor cars, were there?

'Are you suggesting we search Watchcombe for

this Cold Lady?' wailed Milo. He looked miserable. Brewster was similarly forlorn.

'Well, we've got to locate that key,' Kate said. She was finding boys increasingly annoying and unconstructive creatures.

'I think the key is in Mr Mitchell's painting,' suggested Armand.

'Really?' Kate wasn't convinced. 'All he does is paint the sea.'

'Very nicely,' put in Milo.

Armand persisted. 'He also paints the lighthouse a lot. Why? I think it's a clue.'

As they neared the lighthouse, Armand cooed triumphantly. 'See! It looked different in the painting – the top of it was glowing.'

'I don't think Mr Mitchell would have got anything wrong,' said Milo loyally. 'Maybe it's been a while since the lighthouse was working.'

The cat sidled past. Brewster growled and snapped at it, and the cat retreated up onto the lighthouse steps.

'Wait!' called Kate, running after it.

The cat turned to her with annoyance. 'I am on patrol,' it hissed through gritted teeth. 'Do something about that dog, would you?'

'But I have something to ask you. Barnabas says you can tell me about the Lord of Winter.'

'Well, I could,' admitted the cat, staring very intently at something only it could see. 'The Lord of Winter is very old and doesn't really belong here.'

'But what is he? I mean...' Kate tried to keep her

eyes off the darkening sky. 'I mean, is it even a he? I can't see…'

'I can't describe the Lord of Winter to you!' The cat sniffed the air disdainfully. 'You can't see the Lord of Winter, not yet. But you can hear him.'

'Nonsense!' Kate protested. 'It's completely silent.'

The cat stared at her pityingly.

So Kate listened. The only sounds were the distant wind, the creaking of the frozen waves… and a giant's footsteps. Coming closer.

'Oh,' said Kate.

The cat nodded. 'Better hurry up and find that key before he gets here,' it said.

'Come with us,' she said.

The cat shook its head. 'I won't, thanks. Don't like the dog.' It trotted away.

They looked around the lighthouse without success.

'This,' said Kate, 'was not a good idea.'

Armand was unperturbed. 'Well, Mitchell also paints a lot of the nearby coves.'

Kate pointed out that she didn't really fancy climbing over frozen rocks looking for a magic key.

'I don't think we have to,' said Armand, simply. 'You and I are here because we're associated with the objects.'

'I'm not,' wailed Milo. 'I'm from Leighton Buzzard.'

'Ah yes,' Armand was patient. 'But you were sleeping on a beach. Maybe that's where the key is.'

Comprehension dawned in Kate's eyes. 'So we just have to search the beach where Milo was sleeping?' She suddenly thought Armand was quite clever.

Milo burst into tears. 'I can't remember where it was!' he cried.

They headed out of Watchcombe. Armand offered to punch Milo until he remembered where he'd been. Kate did not think this was quite so clever.

The children split up, roving across the various headlands, trying to recognise the beach from Milo's memories. After what seemed an age, Milo gave a shout, popping his head up over the headland. 'I think... I think it's this one!'

They ran to him, scrambling down the hill path to the beach. Here, out of the snow and the wind, it almost seemed like summer again. They trod over iced rock pools clustered with frozen jellyfish. Brewster would pause and lick the occasional pond. The pebbles of the beach were frozen under foot. It was lethally hard to keep upright.

'I'm sure... I'm sure this is it!' exclaimed Milo. Brewster yapped excitedly.

Armand looked at Kate. He seemed nervous.

'Is anything wrong?' Kate asked him.

He shook his head. 'No... I don't think so. I just don't like it here very much.'

Kate shrugged. 'We don't have much choice.'

Armand looked around them. 'Do you know what the locals call this place? Skull Cove.'

Kate's eyes drifted around at the rocks above them. Two small caves high up… and another at ground level. If you squinted, it did look a little like a skull.

'Coo,' said Milo. 'I never saw that. Wow. Those caves would make smashing hiding places.'

'I don't like them,' said Armand. He seemed nervous.

'Well, true – those high-up ones look like an awful risky place to hide something. But what about the mouth? That seems easy enough. Let's go inside!'

'Steady on,' Kate put out a hand. 'You're younger than us, so you should stay outside. With Brewster. I don't want you getting into trouble. If anything happened to you, I'm not sure I could face being banned from Leighton Buzzard.'

Milo protested.

Armand looked glum. 'You want us to go into the cave?'

Kate tutted. It wasn't quite the same as a sigh, so it seemed allowable. 'Fine, scaredy-cat. I'll go on my own. You just look after Milo and Brewster. And if something attacks me, I'll try to keep my screams reasonably quiet.'

She was quite pleased with that, although, as she stepped towards the cave mouth, she felt a wave of panic rising in her. It was just so dark. And really did look like a mouth. Even a normally trickling stream was frozen into a snake's tongue. Her boots crunched on it.

Kate pulled out the torch she'd brought with her,

and it flickered over the roof of the mouth. Thankfully there were no stone teeth clamping down on her, but it was all very oppressive.

She took another step and another. She kept talking to Armand and Milo, but the sound of her voice echoed back to her. She glanced back to the boys, and they seemed suddenly so far away. If she did panic, if something did happen to her, could she reach them in time?

She made herself take another step forward, wishing she had the cat with her. But Kate was alone. Utterly alone, completely —

She heard a noise ahead of her and something brushed her hand. Someone else was in the cave with her. She heard it make a groan, and that was quite enough. She turned, beginning to run, run out of the cave, back to safety.

Which was when she found that something was running into the cave towards her. A terrible, snarling beast.

Chapter
6

Kate gasped in horror. The creature bearing down on her was Brewster, but somehow terribly transformed – slavering jaws and mad staring eyes. She backed away, crying out for help, and felt the torch knocked from her hand by the impact of the dog.

Ordinarily Brewster was quite an unassuming little dog. But now it was just a whirl of teeth and anger.

'Help!' she called, hoping for Milo, or even Armand to come to her rescue – but she could see no one at the cave mouth. Kate was on her own. The dog lurched towards her, and she fell backwards, the breath knocked out of her. All of her stung, the dog on her before she had a chance to get her senses back.

She felt something flowing down her neck. Oh,

she thought, I've been bitten, I'm dying. And then she realised it was drool from the dog.

Brewster darted back, ready for another go. It reared up to spring, and as the dog did so, Kate grabbed the cave wall and launched herself towards the leaping hound.

The soles of her shoes caught Brewster, sending him spinning backwards, slipping helplessly on the ice.

Kate dragged herself up and ran past the dog, who was shaking himself with confusion. She pelted past him, making for the beach. She broke out into the meagre daylight.

'Milo! Armand?' she called. 'It's Brewster! He's gone mad!' But her voice echoed back off the empty beach. The boys had vanished.

Behind her she could hear snarling.

With no time to make for the path, she started to clamber up the cliff face, her bare hands already needle-numb from the cold. Brewster snapped at her heels, spurring her on. She made it to a little ledge, halfway up.

There was still no sign of Milo or Armand.

There was also no going back now. She inched her way along the ledge, reaching the side of the Skull Cove. Here there was a narrow path, little more than a track for rainwater, but it made the ascent slightly easier. By now the pain in her hands was biting – the higher she climbed, the more exposed it became and the colder she got. She shook her head and pulled herself on, further and higher, until she flopped over the top of the cliff. Her coat was cut by thorns, her hair was a mess and she was panting like she'd done cross country. But she felt an enormous sense of achievement.

When she stood up, she saw Armand and Milo standing there watching her.

'There you are!' she said, relieved. 'Where did you go to? What happened to Brewster to upset him so?'

The two boys continued to watch her, blankly.

'Something spooked him. One of you had better be brave enough to go and calm him down – I'm not up to it.' She gave a little laugh.

Neither of the boys laughed.

'What's wrong?' she asked them. 'What's happened? Milo?'

Milo stared at her, his eyes wide.

Her suspicions aroused, she turned on Armand. And she noticed something. He was nervous. Shaking. Afraid.

'What?' she said. 'What have you done? You've done something horrible, haven't you, Armand Dass? It's just like you to let me down.'

Armand shook his head, slightly.

'No.'

The firmness of Milo's voice startled her. The little boy with the golden curls and the simple smile was transformed. His simple smile was now thin and cruel, his blue eyes no longer sparkled.

'What's happened?' she demanded. 'What's Armand said to you?'

'Nothing,' smirked Milo. 'Well, nothing except that he was only too happy to obey me. You see... Armand and I have an agreement. He has been working for me. He doesn't even like you. I made him pretend.' He grinned. 'You thought you had a friend. Two friends. You don't. You're all alone. In my world.'

'*Your* world?' Kate was baffled.

'My lovely world.' Milo giggled. 'I painted it. My name is Milo Mitchell.'

As Kate stared at the little boy, his features changed and shifted again, his body growing taller, his hair uncurling, the golden hue going grey. The skin on his face sagged and wrinkled, but the eyes still danced blue.

Milo Mitchell was suddenly Mr Stevens, the pharmacist.

Armand took a step back. Kate would have as well, but she'd have fallen off the cliff.

'Isn't it lovely?' the old man laughed. 'Oh, it's been jolly fun being young again,' he rubbed his hands. 'Now, I bet you both have questions.'

Kate opened her mouth, but the man held up a hand.

'I can guess! Yes, my real name is Milo Mitchell. Yes, I painted all those pictures, so very long ago. Yes, I was just a little boy. And yes, I was very talented.'

'But you're so old now!' protested Kate.

Mr Mitchell's smile faded slightly. 'Perhaps, perhaps I am.' He sat down on a rock. 'My old limbs feel the cold so. But look at this!' Milo flung an arm around at the world. 'This is the day I made Summer Fall.'

He patted the rocks. 'Come, sit down. I'll tell you.' He paused.

They sat down, and Mr Mitchell started to speak. Kate decided he rather liked being the centre of attention.

'It's a lovely story. When I was young, I was always painting, painting, painting. I used to paint on things I found washed up on the beach – driftwood, sides of tea chests, normally. But then, one day, I was out with friends and we found something on the shore – a sort of canvas or gabardine, but like tin foil. It felt strange to the touch. There was nothing else to hand, so I sat in Skull Cove and I painted on the sheet.

'It was the end of summer, but I imagined how the town had looked in winter. My friends danced around me, ignoring me, chasing each other. Until their cries silenced. And I realised that it had started to snow. In August. The more I painted, the more the snow fell. At first my friends were delighted – then they were frightened. I stopped painting, but it carried on snowing. I tried rubbing the painting out, but it still snowed. Until the whole town had frozen over and the world stopped. Empty apart from my friends and I.

'That was when the Lord of Winter came. He swept across the sea to us. He spoke to me then. He promised me I could live in that day forever. And I stepped forward to agree – but some of my friends stopped me. They were just girls.'

Kate frowned

'But,' Mr Mitchell went on, 'they were strange girls from old families. They shouted at the sky, used weird words, and the more they spoke, the angrier the Lord of Winter became. They hacked at the canvas, the three of them. One tore off a strip and wore it as a band. The other fashioned the foil into a key. The third seized the picture. I tried to grab at them, but the wind howled, and the Lord of Winter screamed... and the snow faded away and it was summer again.

'They took my painting, the ring and the key home to their parents. The elders of the town told me that the Lord of Winter had been waiting outside the town for a very long time, and that I'd found his shield. They said I had summoned an old, dark force by accident, and I wasn't to feel bad about it.

'But I hated them. I painted the same picture, over and over. And nothing happened. I longed for the fall of Summer. But it never happened. A war came. All the boys went away to fight in it. But not me. I stayed here and painted. None of them every came back, and suddenly that long ago magical day seemed more important than ever.

'And those girls who'd stopped me, they didn't understand – they sent me feathers and called me a coward.

'So I went away. I fought in that terrible war. And, somehow, I survived. I'd like to think that the Lord of Winter watched over me. But I was never the same again. Childhood seemed such a long way away.

'I moved away, and I waited. Such a long time. Until my Lord said I could come back.

'And I was only too happy to. As a twinkling old man, running a little pharmacy. It was perfect. All those girls who'd called me names – they were old now. Old and frail. They didn't recognise me when they came in and I handed over their medicines.' He smiled. 'Oh, it was ever so easy to shift the blame onto my assistant.'

'Mr Dass!' said Kate.

Armand flushed and looked at the ground.

'Indeed,' said Mr Mitchell. 'That's why Armand is so eager to help me. Just like his father. He is afraid I will fire him, but I'm only too happy to keep him on, only too happy. After all, he's taken all of the blame for my crimes.'

Armand glared at Mr Mitchell. It was a look of bitter hatred. The old man just laughed.

'We have an understanding.'

Kate found Mr Mitchell baffling, even for an adult. 'So you killed your friends?'

'Happily. They'd ruined my fun. And they sent me feathers...' His voice took on a childish tone. 'I had to get my painting back, didn't I? I didn't know who had it, but it was bound to turn up – after they'd gone. Still, all done now.' Mr Mitchell smiled brightly, as if he was dismissing a mildly disagreeable trip to the dentist.

'What happens next?' asked Kate.

Mr Mitchell sat back on the rock. 'We have to find that key. Once we have, the shield will be complete, and the Lord of Winter can rule forever!'

'But why?' asked Kate. 'I mean, you've explained your plan very neatly. But what is in it for me? At the moment, nothing.'

'But, don't you want to be my friends?' Mr Mitchell looked surprised. 'We can stay here and be children always. It's peaceful. It's beautiful. There are no grown-ups telling you what to do. And what would you rather have it be? Choose Kate – the last week of the school holidays or a Christmas day forever?'

'It's not my decision,' said Kate.

'Oh, but I'd like you to have a say, both of you,' Mr Mitchell adopted a cajoling tone. 'You've helped me. You brought the Lord of Winter back. You've made all this.'

Strictly speaking, Kate thought, a cat did all this, but she doubted that was helping.

'Sure,' she said, and then, 'All right.' A pause. 'Right then. Big decision.'

'Yes?' Mr Mitchell looked like there wasn't much contest.

The pause hung in the air. Armand did not meet her eyes.

'Tell you what,' said Kate, 'I'll get back to you.'

And she ran away.

Kate looked over her shoulder. For a moment, it seemed as though Armand would follow her. But he stood his ground.

So, she was in trouble and on her own. Normally

she despaired of grown-ups. They were lazy, or messy, or rude or unhelpful. But right now, she really very much wanted a grown-up. She wanted to run back to the house and find her mother, and cry until her mother gave her a hug and got her a hot water bottle and put a tin of beans on the stove. Her mother's drawbacks as a cook were normally a source of some irritation to Kate. Kate had made it her business to learn at an early age the secret of omelettes, soufflés and roasts. But right now she wanted very much a plate of her mother's lukewarm beans on cold toast.

She ran on along the cliff face, feeling the wind salty on her face – and then she realised. They were her tears. This was no good. She needed to change tactic. She crouched down behind a gorse bush at the cliff edge and watched. There was no sign of Armand or of Mr Mitchell. But they were somewhere between her and town. And, if she was going to get an advantage, she needed to get past them. She needed to find that key.

Right now, she was stuck. She needed a way to get past them. An alternative.

Kate thought about it, frowning until an idea was pressed into being. If she could climb down to the beach, she could go round the boys simply by making her way across the frozen sea.

There were at least two disadvantages to this that she could think of, but it seemed like a good enough plan.

Kate pushed herself over the headland, took

her gloves off to improve her grip, and started to clamber down the rocks. All went well for the first few handholds, and then she stopped.

New problems presented themselves. It was growing dark, and she couldn't really see beneath her. It was so cold her hands were numb and slipping against the snow. She was far enough down that clambering back up seemed an impossibility, but going on seemed even worse.

She slithered down another few feet, her shoes resting on a narrow ledge that criss-crossed the slope. She heard a light skittering of stones as she shifted her weight onto the ledge.

Kate breathed out quietly. So far, so good. If she kept this up, she would —

The ledge gave way, and Kate slipped down the cliff face.

Her legs kicked out helplessly, finding nothing to grip against. In desperation, one hand grabbed another of the little ledges, and somehow held, jerking the rest of her body with a painful snap.

Kate gasped and then gasped again. She threw another hand onto the ledge, and then, gingerly, tapped her feet along the rocks until one foot found purchase.

She was very, very frightened. She was cold. She was miserable. She was about to fall.

Chapter

7

Kate hung helplessly from the side of the cliff.

And then something tutted.

A small furry head poked over the side of the ledge, stared at her unblinkingly, and then nuzzled her grazed hand.

'Hmm,' said the grey cat. 'How funny.'

'It is not funny,' Kate grizzled, voice thick with tears.

'It is from where I'm sitting,' replied the cat.

'Help me,' she begged.

The grey cat shrugged. 'Sure,' it offered. 'Are you hungry? If so, there's a little nest of voles just over there. I could get you one if you want.'

'No,' Kate said tightly. 'No, thank you.'

'Oh, but I insist. I won't hear another word.' The

cat trotted away.

Kate reflected. Her miserable situation was about to made worse by having vermin dropped on her. She cast around for a lower foothold. It was now so dark she was doing this by feel alone. But what if she simply found a clump of mud and put her entire weight on that? Would the fall kill her? She risked a glance to see how high up she was, and wished she hadn't.

Something small and brown tumbled squeaking past her.

'Oops.' The cat's face appeared over the ledge. 'You missed it. Not to worry. I'll get you another. Just try and catch better this time.'

'No!' Kate shouted at the cat. 'I'm stuck. I can't see a way down. I'm in terrible danger. It's hopeless. Help me.'

Barnabas's cat considered her, unblinkingly. It looked about to say something and then stuck a paw up and cleaned it thoroughly.

'Goodness me,' it said eventually. 'You people do get yourselves in such messes.'

'Please!' Kate was painfully aware of how tired her hands were.

'Tricky,' said the cat. And vanished.

Kate clung to the side of the rock. She was starting to shake – whether from cold or fear, she didn't know.

Something brushed against her leg. She glanced down.

It was the cat. Rubbing against her ankle.

'You silly food-bringer,' it said. 'There's a perfectly good ledge here.'

'I couldn't see it,' Kate protested, shifting her feet onto it gratefully.

'I know,' sighed the cat. 'Humans have such limited eyesight. A little hunting would help you no end. Put your hand there. And – ah yes – there.'

With the cat's help, Kate clambered and slid down the slope, at last feeling her boot crunch into the snow. The cat weaved around her feet.

'That took such a long time,' it yawned. 'I have things to do.'

'Do you now?' Kate scratched it between the ears.

'Oh, all right, then,' it purred. 'I've got time enough for a little fuss.'

'Don't leave me,' she told the cat. 'I could do with the company.'

'Hmm.' The cat closed both of its eyes. 'Will there be biscuits at the end of it?'

'Yes. If I can find any.'

'And warmth?'

'Yes. I'm going to try and get summer back.'

The cat opened an eye. 'And will there be hunting?'

'Oh, absolutely,' said Kate. 'The biggest hunt I've ever been on.'

'It's a deal.'

Kate made for the sea, but the cat stopped her.

'Not that way,' it said. 'There's something I want to show you.'

It led her to the back of the tiny cove, springing from rock to rock until it brought her to a single stone, alone and tall at the front of the beach, just proud of the cliff.

'They call this the Frozen Witch,' the cat said. 'When the tide is high, they talk about the Witch being blind.'

Kate shuddered. 'Was it a real witch, once?'

'They say she was the first to stop the Lord of Winter.' The cat rubbed against the stone.

'The Cold Lady!' Kate cried, remembering the poem. 'Something about her eyes being opened – like now, when the sea is frozen. The key's hidden here.'

'Ah,' said the cat. 'Come here...'

It led her around the back of the Frozen Witch. There was a thin crack in the rock wall. It led into another cave.

'Hurry,' said the cat. 'There's someone waiting for us in here.'

'What?' Kate was alarmed.

'Oh, don't worry. Fairly sure he doesn't want to eat you.' It sniffed the air. 'He doesn't smell hungry.'

They edged through the narrow dankness. It was almost completely dark now, and their path was almost totally obscured.

'You'll have to guide me,' said Kate, feeling her way with her fingertips.

'Honestly,' sighed the cat. 'Must I do everything?'

But it led her on. The way narrowed until Kate thought she'd have to give up. The cave walls pressed in around her.

'Oh,' she said. 'I can still hear the sound of the sea

in here. Funny that.'

The cat did not reply.

At the very narrowest point, the cave suddenly opened out. She squeezed through into a vast, dark space. Her footsteps echoed and crunched.

'Hello...?' she called out. Her voice echoed back.

And then, all of a sudden —

A match was struck.

A face loomed out at her.

Chapter

8

'Hello you!'

It was Barnabas, the museum curator. His voice was muffled.

'Oh!' Kate exclaimed. 'You took your time getting here.'

'And you're a very ungrateful girl.' Again Barnabas's voice was muffled.

'You're just in time, though,' she said. 'We're in terrible danger.'

'Well,' Barnabas sounded regretful. 'I'd love to help, but my hands are tied. Literally.'

'What?'

'A little boy hit me over the head and tied me up.' Barnabas sounded quite resentful. 'He seemed quite nice too.'

Kate went over to him, and started at the ropes holding him. 'I've never been any good with knots,' she said.

'Just try your best. He did gag me as well, but I've managed to do a little about that,' Barnabas said.

Kate worked, marvelling at how long the Curator's match burned. It was clamped in his hands and gave her just enough light to see how to undo the knots.

'No good,' sighed Kate, and started reaching around for a stone or something to cut the ropes. Instead her hand closed on something cold and metal. Perhaps a rusty fork left behind by a picnicker. She hacked away at the Curator's bonds with it.

Then she stopped.

'Carry on!' Barnabas urged.

'But,' protested Kate, 'it's the key! This is it!' She held it up. It glinted bronze by the light of the match.

'Coo,' said the Curator.

'So that's what the poem meant about the Cold Lady.'

'I did wonder,' Barnabas said.

'I don't know if it is a key after all. More like an arrow,' Kate considered.

'Hmm,' agreed Barnabas. He stroked it with a hand. 'Feels funny... From the same bit of material. Well, well done.'

The cat climbed up the cave and dangled its tail in Barnabas's face. 'Geroff,' murmured Barnabas.

'Shan't,' said the cat, and turned around three times on the Curator's head before settling down to sleep.

Kate sawed steadily through Barnabas's bonds with the key and took the gag off. She regarded him.

'Was it you – about an hour ago?' she asked.

'What? In the cave? Yes. I was gagged. I was trying to warn you about the dog.'

'Ah,' said Kate. 'What were you doing in the cave?'

'Um,' said Barnabas. 'I was scrambled. I came looking for you, and I met this charming little tyke. He asked me to look at something he'd seen in a cave and THUD!'

'That,' Kate said crossly, 'was Milo. He's really Milo Mitchell. And also Mr Stevens, the pharmacist.'

'Really?' Barnabas looked interested. 'And he's been wandering around here as a little boy?'

'Yes,' Kate sounded cross. 'Which is impossible. And therefore wrong.'

'Not necessarily. Strange things have been happening here for a long time.' Barnabas lifted the cat off his head and slung it over his shoulder. He started to crunch across the stones, leading them out into Skull Cove. 'We've a lot to do in a very short time, and I shouldn't let a bit of magic worry you.'

'Magic?' Kate snorted. 'There's no such thing. Is there?'

'Magic?' Barnabas shrugged. 'Why not? Magic is cool.'

'But there has to be a rational explanation.'

'Oh there is,' Barnabas led her out of the cave and back to the shore. The frozen sea stretched before them. 'But a rational explanation is rather complex.

We're dealing with a psycho-temporal entity manifesting through a critical mass of its sentient shell... um. Magic sounds more fun.'

'You have a talking cat,' Kate pointed out. 'There's no logical explanation for that.'

The grey cat yawned. 'Yes there is. I've been spending too much time sleeping in his shed,' it said.

'There we are then,' said Barnabas. 'Magic. Now then, let's walk on the sea.'

He took her hand and the two of them stepped onto the waves.

Chapter

9

Kate considered walking on the sea to be an entirely curious experience. It was just as slippy as skating on a frozen lake, but made harder by the frozen waves – forcing them to clamber and slide. The grey cat trotted along beside them, springing from one crest to the next.

'The good thing about this,' grunted Barnabas, 'is that it gives us cover from the town.'

'The bad thing,' Kate winced, grazing her shin on a frozen starfish, 'is that it's quite slow.'

'Yes.'

'We still have to get the painting.'

The Curator smiled at that. 'The important thing is the key. That can either stabilise or banish the Lord of Winter.'

'If only we knew how.' Kate looked at the lowering sky.

'Oh yes,' Barnabas agreed. 'Tricky that.'

They trudged on, inching towards the harbour. Behind them, the giant frozen waves shivered, and the sky grew darker. The creaking increased.

'We are running out of time,' said Barnabas. 'The Lord of Winter is coming.'

'But what is the Lord of Winter? In English.'

Barnabas considered. 'The memory of something old and powerful that shouldn't be here. And wasn't. Until Mr Mitchell found its shield. And the shield remembered its owner and brought him back to life.'

'Is that possible?'

'Magically? Yes.' The Curator grinned. 'And we're going to use the same magic to defeat it before it's too late.'

There was a loud groan behind them. In the distance, giant waves grew dark and shattered as the great shadow swallowed them.

'I think,' announced Kate, 'that now may be too late.'

'This'll be fun,' said the cat.

They broke into a run.

As they ran, the sea shivered and shuddered. In the distance, vast towers of ice toppled and fragmented, ruins skittering across the splintering waves. The cinereous sky pressed in around them.

The darkness was at their backs, and the harbour seemed no closer.

Behind them came a sound like giant's footsteps, and the ice shook and cracked, sheets of it rearing up like behemoths.

Kate made a list of things she liked about this. It was a very short list. She just kept staring at Barnabas's heels. She made herself keep going.

A crack jagged across the sea in front of her, a sudden pit that she toppled into.

The Curator spun round, shot out a hand, and pulled her across the chasm.

'It feels…' she gasped, 'like the end of the world.'

Barnabas grinned. 'I know! The fun bit.'

They ran from the chaos towards the harbour steps. Around them the boats creaked, buckling under the tearing ice. The wind chittered through the masts.

Another chasm zagged open in front of them. The cat leapt over it. Barnabas picked up Kate and tossed her across, her legs slipping on the ice on the other side. As she landed, she heard a yell behind her, and turned in time to see Barnabas vanishing down the hole. The ice closed around him, jaws clamping around his body. Kate ran back to him, but he waved her away. 'No time!' he gasped, as the sea pressed in. 'Get on.'

'But…'

'I'll be fine,' he said. Kate did not think that he looked fine, but sometimes adults said things that were not true.

She turned towards the lighthouse and ran. The cat hesitated, uncertain whether it was more interested in her, or in Barnabas slowly vanishing beneath the frozen waves. Then it followed her.

Kate edged up the harbour steps as quickly as she could, ignoring the lack of a handrail, ignoring the dizzying drop to the ice below. The cat trotted easily behind her.

'Well, there you are,' said a voice. 'We've been waiting.'

Standing by the lighthouse was Mr Mitchell and a snarling Brewster. At their side was a cowed-looking Armand.

Kate considered what to do or say, and used a trick of her mother's – she only acknowledged the person she found least annoying.

'Hello Armand,' she said. 'You look cold.'

Armand nodded miserably.

'Don't worry,' said Kate. 'It's not too late.'

Mr Mitchell, annoyed at being ignored, laughed loudly. 'Hah!' he snarled. 'Happily it is, I tell you it is. I've summoned him and he's coming. Look!'

He pointed up to the sky. And there, pouring out of it, from the horizon, from the sea, was the Lord of Winter.

Chapter
10

Later, Kate tried to describe the Lord of Winter. She couldn't. Or at least, she couldn't without the urge to run from the room and scream. In the end she made a list.

Big.
Dark.
Claws.
Eyes.
Lots of Eyes.
'Wowser,' hissed the cat.

The Lord of Winter spoke, like ice splintering, or the wind on the coldest day. 'You called and I came,' it said. 'Who summoned me?'

'I did!' said Mr Mitchell. 'I want it to be the perfect day for ever.'

'And so it shall be,' the voice promised. 'I give you winter.'

Mr Mitchell smiled. It was not a nice smile.

'Wait a minute,' Kate's voice cut across the storm. She shouted, stopping the wind from snatching her words away. 'Excuse me,' she said, 'I think you'll find that I summoned you, actually.'

'That's a lie!' protested Mr Mitchell.

'No it isn't,' Kate spoke hotly. 'Mr Mitchell may have wanted to, but I did it – I just didn't intend to, that's all. It was more of an… accident.'

The whole sky frowned. The many, many eyes turned to Mr Mitchell.

'Then I am afraid,' it boomed, 'the decision is yours no longer.'

'No,' cried Mr Mitchell. 'I possess two of the three. Surely —'

'The girl summoned me. And she carries the key. That which governs the others.' The Lord of Winter sounded impatient. 'We should abide by the rules.'

'Rules?' Kate pulled out the key and waved it at Mr Mitchell. 'See?' she said.

Mr Mitchell made to snatch it.

Armand blocked his way, gripping his hand. 'No,' he said. 'It's Kate's decision. Let her decide.'

Mr Mitchell knocked him to the ground. Armand grabbed him, and the old man and the boy rolled in the snow. Kate stepped quickly forwards and stared into the sky. The sky stared back at her.

'Well,' demanded the Lord of Winter. 'There is not long. What is it to be?'

'Firstly,' said Kate, 'what's in it for you?'

'Honestly?' The sky laughed. 'I have drifted for so long. Now I shall have a home.'

'I see,' she said eventually. 'Then what is in it for me?'

'Give me the world... and I will give you this town and this day, and you can enjoy it always. You won't grow old, or grow up. The snow will always fall. You'll have no cares. It will always be perfect.'

'What about my mother?' Kate asked.

Hundreds of eyes narrowed a little. 'Would you miss her?'

'Well...' Kate found herself considering the question. It was an interesting one. All her mother did was sleep and be cooked for. Without her, Kate would have a lot less tidying up to do. She glanced at the snow-covered town. It was all so peacefully neat. Like someone had taken the real world and added a lot of straight lines and blank pages.

Actually, she rather liked it.

Mr Mitchell stood up. 'Ha!' he gloated. 'I knew you'd come round.'

'I'm thinking about it,' Kate admitted. She turned back to the staring sky. 'What if I refuse to let you stay?'

The voice rumbled sadly. 'As I go, this tiny little pocket will collapse.'

Out at sea, the mountains of ice fell and tumbled.

'You have not got long,' prompted the voice.

'And if I say no... well, I will be all right, won't I?' she said. 'I can go home?'

'Ah.' The sky smiled nastily at her. 'If I lose my hold on this world, I won't go home empty-handed.'

'Is that a threat?'

The sky shrugged. 'Merely a possibility.' It paused. 'Place the three objects together, and my shield will be complete. I can step into this world. And then there will be perfect order. For ever.'

'Or…?'

'Turn the key in its lock and we will fall together.'

'Where is the lock?'

'I need hardly tell you that,' coaxed the Lord of Winter. 'You won't need it.'

'No,' admitted Kate. 'No, I won't.'

Kate took a deep breath. The snow drifted down, the sea continued to crumble, and Armand and Mr Mitchell looked on. Armand looked worried. Mr Mitchell looked triumphant.

This was the moment.

There was a polite little cough.

'Made up your mind?' asked the grey cat. 'Only, you're running out of time.'

'Oh yes,' said Kate. And ran forward.

Kate hurled herself at the steps up to the lighthouse. Behind her she heard Mr Mitchell's shout of anger. He let go of Brewster's leash.

Kate raced up the spiral stairs around the lighthouse, skidding and slipping against the iced metal. Her hands wouldn't grip on the frozen handrail. Behind her the hound growled at her feet.

To start with it made her climb faster and

faster. But then she ran out of breath. And still the dog bounded up the steps, ironwork echoing its thundering gait. Snarling as it got closer.

She took another step before the animal pounced. Its jaws snapped at her face. She backed away, pressing against the railing. She threw her arms up, fighting to keep her balance. The dog snarled and leapt again.

She could hear her screams. She could hear the dog's hatred.

But worse, she could hear the Lord of Winter laughing.

It was a long way down. A long way up to the distant glow of the lamp at the top of the lighthouse. She was petrified and the dog showed no signs of giving up. She flailed out with the key, but the dog simply seized on it like a stick, tugging it away from her. She knew she'd made a mistake and didn't dare let go.

Nor did she dare push back as the dog's jaws worried at the key, jerking her off balance. Kate suddenly felt very small and alone.

She could see Mr Mitchell, his face triumphant.

She could see Armand, worried and sad.

And, in the distance, out at sea, she could see Barnabas, pulling himself out of the ice, staring at her, waving and shouting. He had such a nice face, she thought. A good last thing to see.

Kate closed her eyes and got ready to fall.

Then she heard it. A screaming howl and a yap from the dog. She opened her eyes.

The grey cat was locked in a struggle with Brewster, a whirl of claws and fur. Brewster let go of the key, turning to clamp down on the cat. The cat howled, hissing and spitting at the dog. The two tore back and forth across the narrow steps.

'Hurry!' yowled the cat. 'You're running out of time…'

'But, but…' said Kate.

'Hurry!' the cat hissed, leaping up onto the handrail, then plunging onto the dog. Brewster jumped up to meet it, and the cat swiped sideways, wrapping a tail around the dog's face.

The cat landed, spun and turned, puffing itself up into a large, angry spiky greyness. It let out a wailing howl of warning. The dog gulped out breath and drool and then bounded for the cat. It smacked into it, carrying both of them over the side of the lighthouse.

Kate watched them tumble down for a second then turned away before the loud thud.

She was crying, but she carried on running.

She made the last ten steps. At the top of the lighthouse the wind was fierce, plucking at her hair and skin.

The wind grew. Out at sea the last of the mountains collapsed, melting away like ice cubes in squash. The terrible dark face of the Lord of Winter leered down at her.

'You are out of time! This little realm is nothing, a stepping stone to your home… Give me the key, little girl.'

Kate smiled at the Lord of Winter, feeling the icy breath cut into her. She stretched out her hand, thrusting the key onto the top of the little light, fitting it neatly into a slot. She turned the object. At last she saw what it was. A key, yes, an arrow, perhaps... but really it was a weathervane.

The little gold dart spun in the wind.

The lamp glowed and burned out into the world. The Lord of Winter glared at Kate with all of its many, many eyes. Then it screamed.

Light poured from its mouths and its eyes, the clouds snapped down, and the world broke apart and stopped.

Chapter

11

The world started again.

Kate was lying on the platform at the top of the lighthouse. A patch of clear blue sky burned through the clouds. The sun was warm against her frozen skin. She sat up.

Feet thundered up the metal steps and Armand ran to her, helping her up. Behind him came Barnabas, holding something in his arms. At first she thought it was a coat.

Then she realised.

It was the body of the grey cat.

'Oh,' said Kate.

She ran towards Barnabas. 'Do something!' she yelled.

He shook his head, sadly offering her the bundle in his arms.

She cradled the cat, and its eyes flickered open.

'Ah,' it said. 'Hello.' It tried to lick a paw, but gave up and blinked at her. 'It's nice and warm up here,' it said. 'Finally.'

Kate looked up. The patch of blue sky was spilling out. The clouds hurried away, almost embarrassed. A shaft of sunlight shone down, glinting off the weathervane.

'Winter is over,' said Barnabas sadly. 'The sun is coming out.'

'I see.' The cat made a feeble effort to nudge Kate under the chin. It gave up. 'So, this is what death feels like. I had wondered. Interesting.' Its whiskers twitched. 'Could you hold me up to the sunlight, please? I'd like to feel the heat.'

Kate did so, her hands stretching up as far as they could. 'Nice,' muttered the cat, and yawned.

'No!' sobbed Kate.

'I'm afraid so,' said the cat. 'I am so terribly, terribly tired.'

Its eyelids flickered and steadily drew shut. The grey cat purred away to itself for a while, and then went silent.

Kate held out the still bundle until her arms ached, and then Barnabas took it gently from her.

'I'm sorry,' he said.

Kate wiped her nose, and then stepped to the railing. 'Where's Mr Mitchell?' she demanded.

Armand pointed. Mr Mitchell stood there, defiantly on the ground.

'Do what you like!' he roared. 'I'm staying here.'

Barnabas crossed over to the railing and stared down. 'Little boys,' he thundered, 'should not play with toys they're not supposed to.'

'I am not a little boy,' retorted Mr Mitchell, proudly.

'Oh yes you are,' Kate told him. 'You grew old, but you never grew up. It's a shame. You've wasted your life.'

'Come up here,' urged Barnabas. 'This world is falling away and we're going back home. The top of the lighthouse is the only bit that's safe.'

'Safe?' shouted Mr Mitchell. 'Fat chance. I'm staying here.'

'You can't!' said Kate. 'There's still time! The Lord of Winter has gone. Summer is coming back.'

'I don't believe you.' Mr Mitchell was defiant. 'I'll be young again! He can't be defeated by a stupid girl.'

At that point, Kate decided she really didn't care what happened to him.

'I'm staying,' shouted Mr Mitchell.

As he spoke, figures sprang up across the sea. Ghostly figures with young faces. They were in uniform and they were marching silently towards the shore.

'You see?' laughed Milo. 'They're all coming back home. All my friends. We're all going to be young forever! I finally get what I want.'

As he spoke, a crack echoed across the sea. The ghostly figures vanished as the sea split apart, water pouring up from a zigzag, icebergs crashing down towards the harbour. The walls shook under the impact and the lighthouse lurched at an alarming angle. Actually, thought Kate, if you're standing on top of a lighthouse, any angle that isn't perpendicular is alarming.

'Quickly!' yelled Barnabas. 'Grab on to a railing! It's about to get very exciting.'

The lighthouse tipped, falling up into the sun which was suddenly coming towards them very fast.

Chapter

12

The town woke up to a glorious late summer day. At first no one noticed anything amiss. True, over the next few days, keen gardeners were surprised at the early appearance of snowdrops and daffodils.

But no one said anything much. Town gossip was consumed by the surprise disappearance of the pharmacist. At first, many fingers were pointed at Mr Dass, but then, when a constable cycled over from Minehead, a lot of interesting things were found in the storeroom at the back. Suddenly, sheepish men were trying very hard to be nice to Armand's father, while sour-faced ladies said of Mr Mitchell that They Had Always Known.

It was the last Sunday afternoon of summer. Kate had just finished helping her mother string up a hammock in the garden. ('Well, dear, it has such a nice view,' her mother had said, before shutting her eyes and falling asleep.)

Armand stuck his head over the hedge. 'Hello,' he said.

Kate waved back.

'It doesn't seem real,' he said. 'There really will be school tomorrow.'

'I know,' Kate laughed. 'Just think. If it wasn't for me, there'd never be school ever again. Oh.' She frowned. 'I wish I hadn't said that out loud.'

'It might not be that bad,' Armand suggested. 'People might actually talk to me this term. Now they no longer think my father's a poisoner.'

'True,' admitted Kate. 'Puts my problems into perspective. I'll add that to the list.'

'Do that,' said Armand. 'If it helps.'

They stood, looking at each other for a minute.

'It's a nice afternoon,' said Armand. 'We could do something. You know, have a proper nose round the museum. Something pointless and unplanned.'

Kate smiled. 'Yes,' she said. 'I'd like that.'

'Well, only if it's open.'

'I'll go and ask Barnabas.' Kate hadn't seen the Curator for days. He'd been out.

She ran to the side of the garden, past her gently snoring mother, and squeezed herself through the hedge.

Barnabas's garden was empty, grass baking in the afternoon sunshine. The grand old house was quiet. She went round to the back of it, and noticed the candy-striped tent still there. A flap was open. She pulled it back and peeped inside.

The small tent was empty, but a smell hung in the air. The smell of earth after rain. She sniffed and, somehow, oddly, she knew that she would never see the mysterious Barnabas ever again.

She stepped out of the tent, and something moved in the corner of her eye. She turned, just in time to glimpse a cat's tail vanish into the hedge. It was grey.

Heart beating, she made to go after it, but then the bell on Armand's bicycle called to her. She ran down the garden path into the lane.

'Come on,' she said. 'We've only got an afternoon left. Let's make the most of it.'

And they did.

Melody Malone stars in

The Angel's Kiss

by Melody Malone
with Justin Richards

Chapter 1

The Handsome Client

On some days, New York is one of the most beautiful places on Earth. This was one of the other days. The sky was the colour of an old church roof, and the rain was giving stair rods a bad reputation.

Some days you just know things are going to get dangerous and out of hand, and this was without a doubt one of those. About time too.

I was the only person in the office. That wasn't exactly unusual as I was the only employee of the Angel Detective Agency. As the owner too, I can tell you that I didn't think I was doing a good job of keeping the work rolling in. But then the sorts of cases I was interested in were rather specialised. Not your run-of-the-mill cheating spouse and missing cat. Or even missing spouse and cheating cat. No, I was more interested in arcane, eclectic, and other words you probably wouldn't expect a New York private detective to use all that much.

Leaning back in my chair, with my high heels resting on the unpaid bills that cluttered the desk, I listened to the rain beating against the window. Another sound was beating a regular rhythm – feet on the wooden stairs.

Might be the cleaner, I thought. I checked the calendar – 1938. I hadn't planned on cleaning the place until at least 1946. The footsteps paused on the landing outside my office. Maybe they were heading on up to the pet food supplier on the fifth floor. They'd be disappointed if they were, as the company went bust in the Crash. There were starving pets flinging themselves out of windows, or so it was said. I glanced out of the window now, and saw that in a sense it was still raining cats and dogs.

Whoever was loitering outside still hadn't moved on. 'If you're looking for the Angel Detective Agency,' I called out, 'it's through the door marked "Angel Detective Agency".'

If they couldn't work that out, then they'd come to the right place for help.

I caught a reflection of myself in the glass of the door as it opened. Just a flash, as I swung my legs off the desk. Just a quick glimpse to assure myself that everything was buttoned and unbuttoned in the best places and pointing in the right direction.

The dark figure of a man stood in the doorway, barely more than a silhouette. But his voice was promising – deep and dark as his shadow.

'Melody Malone?'

I smiled and pushed my fedora up with my index

finger so he could see the full extent of my brow. 'In the flesh.' I lingered on the noun.

'Can I come in?'

I smiled invitingly. 'When we haven't even been introduced?' But I gestured to a spare chair. There was only one, so he couldn't get lost.

As he sat, his face moved from the shadows into the light cast by my rather inadequate desk lamp. It didn't help that I'd angled the lamp to show off my own assets rather than his. But I quickly remedied that as I caught sight of the square jaw, the carefully slicked hair, the deep blue eyes, and the Clark Gable moustache. Though Gable wouldn't be properly famous for another year, and at that time his moustache was, often as not, a false one...

So it was no big surprise that it wasn't actually Clark Gable sitting in my office. But it was the next best thing. Possibly better.

He reached across the desk to shake hands. His grip was firm and assertive, but then so was mine.

'Miss Malone,' he breathed.

'Rock Railton,' I replied. 'Unless you're his stunt double?' I raised an alluring eyebrow. Alluringly.

'In the flesh,' he replied, lingering on the preposition. He needed to work on that. 'I guess it saves time that you know who I am.'

'I guess it does. But believe me, I have plenty of time. It's the business I'm in.'

Talking of time, about ninety-five per cent of you people reading this can save some right now by skipping on. But for those few who have never heard of Rock Railton, here's a bit of background that had raced through my brain when I recognised the most handsome movie icon working on the East Coast.

That's right – the *East* Coast. I know what you're thinking. This is 1938, so all the studios have upped and moved to Hollywood long ago. All, that is, except Starlight. Or to give the company it's full name: The Starlight Motion Picture Company of America (New York, NY) Inc. Which is probably why it's usually just called Starlight Studios.

Starlight's success was built on its stars rather than the movies it made. Obviously people went to the movies – that was how they made their money. But they didn't go to see the film. They didn't go for the story, or the sets or the costumes. Such as they were. They went to see the *stars*.

There had been reports in the press recently about some of the studio's minor stars defecting to the West Coast studios. No doubt they'd been lured away with lucrative contracts, offers of fame, and the glamour-appeal of Hollywood. It was unlikely they'd get much of any of them, though. Most likely the major studios just wanted them *not* to be working for Starlight. After all, to become a Starlight Star you didn't actually need to be able to *act*.

So I guess it wasn't really a surprise that – if newspapers are to be believed, which of course they are not – so many of the actors (with a small 'a') and actresses (with a large double 'D') didn't seem to have got as far as Hollywood but disappeared somewhere en route. 'En route', in case you don't know, is French for 'got distracted along the way'.

But whatever their thespian talent, Starlight Stars were quite simply the most glamorous, the most cinematic, the most beautiful and handsome in the industry. And just as the most beautiful of the Starlight Starlets was Giddy Semestre, so the most handsome of the Starlight Stars was Rock Railton.

And here he was, sitting opposite me in the dusty offices of the Angel Detective Agency. In the flesh. My own flesh was getting goose bumps just at the thought. Which was slightly embarrassing as so much of it was on display just now.

I leaned back in my chair and adopted an even more nonchalant pose.

'So, how can I help you, Mr Railton?'

'Someone's planning to kill me.' He raised his eyebrows and opened his hands apologetically, as if to say: 'Such a bore, but what can you do?'

'You been to the cops?' I asked. It seemed like a good question.

'No.'

'Are you going to tell me why not?'

He considered this, though I didn't think it was a difficult question. I was saving that up for next. This question had a very limited possible set of answers. 'Boolean' is another word NY PIs don't often use.

'It's complicated,' he decided at last. So not as Boolean as I'd thought, apparently.

'Mr Railton,' I said smokily, '"Complicated" is

my middle name.' Actually, it's not my middle name – any more than Malone is my last name. Whether Melody is really my first name is, well, complicated.

'Sorry.'

I smiled to show I wasn't at all put out. 'So why come to me?'

'Your name,' he said. 'Sounds strange, but it just felt, you know – *apt*.'

'My name? You mean Melody Malone? I only use the "Complicated" on formal occasions,' I clarified.

'The firm's name.'

'The Angel Detective Agency. Why is that apt?'

'Because of the kiss of the angel.' He gave a short laugh at my frown. 'Sorry, I guess that doesn't make a lot of sense.'

'And I guess it's complicated.' But he had me intrigued. Angels, after all, are my business.

'Actually, it's pretty simple,' Railton went on. 'I was at the studio, and I overheard someone planning my death.'

'I take it they weren't talking about a movie.'

He shook his head and the shadows did good things for his profile if not my blood pressure. 'They said I would be dead in a couple of weeks. Then they said something about "the kiss of the angel" and how they already have my replacement lined up.' His movie-star face cracked into despondency. 'It's so unfair – I feel like I only just got started.'

To my knowledge, Rock Railton had been the top Starlight name for at least two years now, but I didn't quibble. In a career where most people's success was measured in weeks, he'd done pretty well for himself.

I stuck to the more obvious. 'So,' I asked, 'who was it you overheard planning to kill you?'

He looked at me with what might have been sympathy, or possibly disappointment. I'm not sure which as I don't go looking for sympathy and I rarely disappoint.

'If I knew that,' Railton said, 'I wouldn't need to hire you.'

'Really?' Time to retrieve the situation. 'It may surprise you to learn that lots of people hire me to tell them things they already know, Mr Railton.' I smiled winningly. 'Things like "Your husband is cheating on you." Or "Your employer is a crook." Then there's "Your cat is almost certainly dead," and "You really shouldn't wear that blouse with those shoes." You're very handsome.'

He blinked. I made a note to warn him about that. 'People hire you to tell them they're handsome?'

'Sorry, no. That was just me getting a bit carried away. Do you ever get carried away, Mr Railton?'

He leaned back in his chair and clasped his hands in front of him. 'You've got some front, you know.'

I made sure the best bits of it were pointing right at him. 'I know.'

'You flirt with all your clients?' he wondered.

'Usually they flirt with me. But I'm pleased to hear you're a client.' I leaned across the desk. 'You *are* my client, aren't you, Mr Railton?'

He swallowed as if the full implications of his

visit had only just become apparent to him. Or so I hoped. 'I can pay you a hundred dollars a day.'

I didn't like to say that I'd happily have paid him double that for the case. So I didn't. Instead I said, 'Plus expenses.'

'Will that be much?'

'I'm an expensive lady. But for you, I'll try to hold back a little.'

He smiled. 'Not too much I hope.'

'Not too much,' I agreed.

We talked a little business. Boring stuff that included phrases like 'cash only', and 'meet potential suspects' and, most important of all 'Please, call me Rock.' Then Rock, as I now called him, said that he had to be going, which wasn't something that had featured high on my own agenda, but he would see me at the launch party for his new film tomorrow.

'Lady, don't shoot,' he said.

'As if I could conceal a gun in this,' I told him, standing up so he could get the full benefit of my heels, stockings, skirt, blouse, and everything. Especially the everything.

'Probably true,' he noted. Maybe he could be a detective after all. 'But that's the name of the movie.'

'I'll be there,' I assured him.

'Good title, eh?' His moustache twitched rather fetchingly as he smiled. 'Lady Don't Shoot.'

I smiled back even more fetchingly. 'I'm making no rash promises.'

Chapter 2

Age Before Beauty

Tomorrow was, as a popular movie would later have it, another day. Still damp, but not so wet. Though the rain had eased, the streets were puddled and the sidewalks were sweating. It was the sort of day when deciding what to wear is like planning a military operation. Believe me – I have considerable experience of both.

Fortunately, I like dressing up almost as much as I like dressing down. So I spent a pleasant couple of hours in my apartment with a variety of blouses, skirts, suits, shoes, hats, and – let's face it – lingerie. Plus a mirror. The secret is not just to be stunning, which I find comes rather easily, to be honest. The tricky thing is getting exactly the right level of stun for the occasion.

A launch party for a new Starlight movie was, I reckoned, pretty high on the stun-counter. That said, the trip across New York to get to the party was probably not. A long, stylish raincoat in a fashionable cut, topped off with my favourite fedora therefore completed the ensemble.

I spent a few moments practising my entrance to the event – easing out of the drab grey coat and allowing the imagined guests to behold the contrast of my lovely lace and suggestive net and adorable satin. Quite a few moments, actually.

I've never been very good at looking helpless. But there are times when needs must, and one of those is when you require a cab in the rain. Several gentlemen were kind enough to allow me ahead of them into a taxi. The driver's eyes lingered longer in the rear-view mirror than was strictly necessary as he asked me how far I was going.

'All the way,' I told him, giving the address. I've never been one to resist a single entendre.

'Your accent – you British?' he asked. Perceptive as well as cheeky.

'Only my accent,' I assured him. 'The rest of me is… cosmopolitan.'

He nodded knowingly, swerving round a pedestrian. 'Never been there myself.'

'You have missed so much.'

Evening was drawing in and the cars had their lights on, cutting through the inevitable rain. I watched the drops paint clear lines down the grubby cab windows. We drove in binary fashion – either stop or go. Go fast, and stop was sudden. The journey was punctuated by a liberal use of the horn, presumably to make up for the complete avoidance

He was weakening. 'You said you'd help.' What hope there was faded from his eyes.

'I offered you money,' I corrected him. 'I'm sorry, really I am, but I can't help you turn back time. Not without calling in many more favours than I currently have saved up.'

'You promised.' He was going for my coat again, but I managed to step aside. 'Yesterday,' he went on. 'You promised yesterday that you'd help.'

'Sweetie – I've never seen you before in my life. Or yours.'

Then he really surprised me. He stuffed his hands into his jacket pockets and pulled out handfuls of money. He had small hands, but they were big handfuls. Ten-dollar bills, crumpled and creased as much as his weather-beaten face. He threw the money at me, right there in the street. It blizzarded round my head, caught in the breeze and swirling through the evening. People stopped and gawped and grabbed.

I just watched. Watched the money spin and fall. Watched the last hope fade from the old man's eyes as his knees buckled and he fell to the sidewalk. Watched his hand flop into the gutter where the rainwater running into a storm drain washed the dust and grime from his cuffs.

Under the layers of age and the wrinkles and pockmarks the man was almost unrecognisable. Almost. But I recognised him now. Just as I recognised the suit he was wearing, the pattern and the colour bright and restored where the water rinsed away the

of the indicator lights.

Finally the cab drew up at the kerb with a jerk. The jerk stayed behind the steering wheel as I eased myself out.

'You need a ride later?' he asked, apparently serious.

I found the exact fare and told him: 'Oh, I hope not.' If he wanted a tip, then I was ready with: 'Stop for red lights.' But he didn't comment on the money I handed over and was soon disappearing in a cacophony of horn and brake pads.

Lower East Street was closed to traffic, so he'd dropped me on a nearby corner. The rain had eased, but even so I decided I'd tipped him too much. I turned my collar up and pulled the brim of my hat down before heading towards the venue.

Intriguing case or not, I was looking forward to the party. It was at Nick's which as anyone who is anyone will tell you is *the* place to be seen. Nick's is where millionaires go for breakfast, where top fashion models call in for lunch, and where senators and mafia bosses have to book well ahead if they want a table for dinner.

I could see the awning further down the street. The remains of the rain was running off it at the edges forming a translucent curtain round the red carpet and uniformed doormen. A trickle of well-dressed people flowed under the awning, doing their best to avoid being dripped on while maintaining their dignity.

Across the street from Nick's was a small park,

surrounded by iron railings. The statue of a woman and an angelic-looking child, holding hands, stared out across the road and into the front entrance of the restaurant. I watched it for a moment, then looked away. When I looked back, the statue had not moved.

I guess that's what you'd expect. But you can never be too careful. And especially not where statues are involved.

My high heels clicked impressively on the paved sidewalk as I approached Nick's. I paused for a moment to take out a compact and check my make-up in the mirrored lid. Lipstick can be so important when properly applied. It's one of my most formidable weapons. A quick check that my other weapons were properly deployed and I stepped forward again.

Right into the path of a tramp – a hobo – who staggered out of a dark alleyway in front of me. He was obviously headed for a very different destination. Most likely one suffixed with 'gutter'.

That said, he was wearing a nice suit. I had a good view of the herringbone weave of the right sleeve. The suit was torn and stained and about three sizes too big, but I could imagine the old man's elation at finding such a prize discarded in someone else's trash.

The reason I had such a good view of the sleeve was because the old man had grabbed the front of my raincoat. I shuddered to think what he might have been aiming for, but right now he had a handful of

button and weatherproofing clutched in his gnarled, arthritic fingers.

'I knew you'd be here.' His voice was a throaty rasp that sounded like it had been through a cheese grater on its way from his larynx to the outside world.

'Excuse me?' This was both an exclamation of surprise and an escape gambit as I attempted to push past him. The smell was... interesting.

But he still had hold of my coat and, despite his frailty, he wasn't about to let go.

'You have to help me – *please*.'

'All right,' I conceded, reaching for my clutch bag. 'How much?'

He seemed confused for a moment. I know confusion when I see it, and I was looking at it right now.

'I don't...' He paused to cough violently, jolting my raincoat up and down as his chest spasmed. Mine too, under the onslaught. 'I don't want money,' he finally managed to gasp.

Well that was a first. He probably knew confusion when he saw it too.

'I want my life back,' he rasped. 'I used to *be* someone...'

'Didn't we all, honey.'

I finally managed to extract his curled fingers from my coat. Hopefully the wrinkles would drop out in time. From my coat, I mean, not his hands. There was no remedy for them, and the problem was Anno Domini.

dust and the dirt.

It was the same suit that Rock Railton had been wearing when he called on me yesterday and I promised to help him.

Chapter 3
Lady Don't Shoot

I was wrong of course. It was just some tramp who'd had the good fortune to find a suit from the same store where Rock Railton shopped (OK, one with pockets stuffed with cash, but everyone gets lucky sometimes). An old man who was so confused and so close to death that he thought he knew me, that he would ask a stranger for help. He didn't want to die – well, that's hardly a surprise.

Nothing to see here, move right along, please.

I did the helpless thing again and some of the passers-by stopped jumping for ten-dollar bills long enough to realise the old guy needed some help. Or rather, that he was past it.

'Let me through – I'm a doctor.'

My heart beat a little faster, and I lingered just long enough to be sure he'd used the indefinite article. But the man was short and bald and rather ugly – not at all like any Doctor I'd consult. I hope. If 'consult' is the right word.

By the time I reached Nick's I was completely composed again and ready to perform my renowned raincoat removal routine. I assured myself that the statue still hadn't moved, and then caught sight of Rock Railton walking into Nick's ahead of me. Any final doubts or worries I might have had disappeared as quick as the sun in an English summer.

The doorman frowned at me when I introduced myself. 'Miss Malone – you're not on the list.'

'Maybe not your list, sweetie. But I'm on nearly everyone else's.' It didn't take a lot to persuade him to let me in.

Rock had already disappeared deep into the melee of guests. I did the raincoat thing and draped it over the arm of a nearby waiter, not bothering to check how many people had watched. I recognised the sound of jaws dropping.

The waiter holding my coat, and apparently attempting to make eye contact somewhere south of my own jaw, directed me through the large foyer to the ballroom where the party was being held.

Another waiter appeared beside me before I was three steps into room.

He offered up a silver tray of fluted glasses. 'Champagne?'

'I prefer the real thing,' I assured him in a loud whisper. I took a glass anyway and surveyed the room as I sipped. It wasn't bad. But it wasn't very French either.

My plan, such as it was, centred on talking to

Rock Railton and getting an idea of who the likely suspects were. Chances were that whoever wanted him dead was in this room – and I don't just mean the critics.

Everyone was here. I recognised other movie stars, like Giddy Semestre whose neckline was even more pronounced than my own. It didn't so much plunge as plummet. I spotted some big-name producers including Maximilian Schneider dePost von Algonquin – who has to be one of the biggest names in any industry.

Then there was the press. I knew some of the owners of the big papers very well indeed. They fell into two camps – those who smiled and raised their glasses in greeting when they saw me, and those who turned away and tried to hide their faces in the hope I wouldn't recognise or remember them. I could write a few headlines there.

I couldn't for the moment see Rock Railton, so I made my way across the room towards Giddy Semestre. She was the co-star of *Lady Don't Shoot*, and there were rumours that she and Rock were romantically linked. At the hip. Whatever the truth of that, it seemed likely that Rock would gravitate towards Giddy before too long.

Plus it's always nice to talk to the most beautiful and intelligent woman in the room. So Giddy would be grateful for the opportunity.

I reached Giddy and her entourage in time to hear the end of a rather obvious joke and leaned forward in order to steal the punchline.

There was a moment's silence, into which I added: 'Sorry – were you actually telling the version with the minotaur and the ukulele?' Several people drifted away after that and soon I was alone with Miss Semestre.

'I'm sorry, but have we met before?' she asked.

I shook my head. 'I'm sure you'd remember.'

She smiled, raised a perfectly pencilled eyebrow, and looked me up and down. 'I'm sure I would.'

'I'm a friend of Rock Railton.'

'That may not narrow things down very much,' she said.

'Do I look like I need narrowing down?' I wondered. I congratulated her on her performance in the movie. Her smile widened alarmingly as I poured on the praise for her acting abilities.

But she wasn't as dizzy as her name suggested. It was genuine amusement rather than immodesty. 'You haven't actually seen the movie, have you?' she said.

I had to confess that I'd skipped the movie bit and come straight to the party. 'But I'm sure you were very good in it.'

'You can sure lie,' she said, smile still in place. 'But I can't act to save my life. Oh, I have no illusions about that,' she went on before I could pretend to disagree. 'I'm there to look good. And maybe my looks are the best act of the lot.'

I asked her what she meant. Even up this close she wasn't as heavily made-up as most of the women in the room. I'd passed one lady who had arrived well plastered in every sense.

Before she could answer me, a short man with oiled-back thinning hair who looked like he'd needed some of the same oil to ease him into his bulging suit arrived. He smudged the back of Giddy's hand with his greasy lips.

'Darling!' he announced, as if this was a complete conversation. 'Darrr-ling!' he said again – you could practically hear the subject- verb-object construction within those two syllables.

He straightened up from the kiss, though that didn't buy him much height, and looked at me askance. 'Who's your friend?'

Giddy was giving the lie to her comments about her own acting talents by making a good job of hiding her disgust at the guy's slobbering. 'Oh, Max – this is…' She stumbled.

I helped her out. 'Melody Malone.'

'Melody Malone, eh?' He sounded like he reckoned I'd just made the name up. So maybe he was more perceptive than I thought. 'What studio you with?'

'I'm not in the movie business,' I confessed.

He pursed his lips in an especially unpleasant manner. 'You ever decide you should be, give me a call.' He bowed just enough for me to get the full impact of his bald patch. My guess was he didn't know that from this angle he looked like a monk at prayer.

'And you are?' I asked.

That hit him right between the eyes just as

he straightened up. There was a certain amount of spluttering from the Monk-Man, and barely concealed amusement from Miss Gillespie.

'I'm kidding,' I said in my bestest silkiest voice.

He obviously believed I must indeed be joking, and turned to share the amusement with Giddy, allowing me time to give her an exaggerated blank look.

Luckily she realised I hadn't a clue as to his identity and rescued me. I don't often need rescuing, but it's nice when it goes well and doesn't involve great heights.

'Oh, Miss Malone, you're such a tease,' Giddy said. 'Everyone knows Max Kliener, head of Starlight Studios. He produced *Lady Don't Shoot*, of course.'

'Of course.' Well, yes, I'd heard of Kliener. I always thought he sounded like a commercial for an industrial vacuum appliance, and made a mental note to tell him some time. But maybe not just now.

Kliener jabbed a podgy finger at me several times, while looking me up and down and appraising me in a way that seemed particularly unnecessary. 'Had me there,' he said.

'You wish,' I murmured.

'But, like I said – you decide to get into movies, I can find a place for you at Starlight. Just come down to the set any time and ask for Max Kliener. Everyone knows Max.'

I switched on my own oiliest smile. 'You sure about that… Max – was it?'

He exploded with laughter. Well, not literally

of the indicator lights.

Finally the cab drew up at the kerb with a jerk. The jerk stayed behind the steering wheel as I eased myself out.

'You need a ride later?' he asked, apparently serious.

I found the exact fare and told him: 'Oh, I hope not.' If he wanted a tip, then I was ready with: 'Stop for red lights.' But he didn't comment on the money I handed over and was soon disappearing in a cacophony of horn and brake pads.

Lower East Street was closed to traffic, so he'd dropped me on a nearby corner. The rain had eased, but even so I decided I'd tipped him too much. I turned my collar up and pulled the brim of my hat down before heading towards the venue.

Intriguing case or not, I was looking forward to the party. It was at Nick's which as anyone who is anyone will tell you is *the* place to be seen. Nick's is where millionaires go for breakfast, where top fashion models call in for lunch, and where senators and mafia bosses have to book well ahead if they want a table for dinner.

I could see the awning further down the street. The remains of the rain was running off it at the edges forming a translucent curtain round the red carpet and uniformed doormen. A trickle of well-dressed people flowed under the awning, doing their best to avoid being dripped on while maintaining their dignity.

Across the street from Nick's was a small park,

surrounded by iron railings. The statue of a woman and an angelic-looking child, holding hands, stared out across the road and into the front entrance of the restaurant. I watched it for a moment, then looked away. When I looked back, the statue had not moved.

I guess that's what you'd expect. But you can never be too careful. And especially not where statues are involved.

My high heels clicked impressively on the paved sidewalk as I approached Nick's. I paused for a moment to take out a compact and check my make-up in the mirrored lid. Lipstick can be so important when properly applied. It's one of my most formidable weapons. A quick check that my other weapons were properly deployed and I stepped forward again.

Right into the path of a tramp – a hobo – who staggered out of a dark alleyway in front of me. He was obviously headed for a very different destination. Most likely one suffixed with 'gutter'.

That said, he was wearing a nice suit. I had a good view of the herringbone weave of the right sleeve. The suit was torn and stained and about three sizes too big, but I could imagine the old man's elation at finding such a prize discarded in someone else's trash.

The reason I had such a good view of the sleeve was because the old man had grabbed the front of my raincoat. I shuddered to think what he might have been aiming for, but right now he had a handful of button and weatherproofing clutched in his gnarled, arthritic fingers.

'I knew you'd be here.' His voice was a throaty rasp that sounded like it had been through a cheese grater on its way from his larynx to the outside world.

'Excuse me?' This was both an exclamation of surprise and an escape gambit as I attempted to push past him. The smell was... interesting.

But he still had hold of my coat and, despite his frailty, he wasn't about to let go.

'You have to help me – *please*.'

'All right,' I conceded, reaching for my clutch bag. 'How much?'

He seemed confused for a moment. I know confusion when I see it, and I was looking at it right now.

'I don't...' He paused to cough violently, jolting my raincoat up and down as his chest spasmed. Mine too, under the onslaught. 'I don't want money,' he finally managed to gasp.

Well that was a first. He probably knew confusion when he saw it too.

'I want my life back,' he rasped. 'I used to *be* someone...'

'Didn't we all, honey.'

I finally managed to extract his curled fingers from my coat. Hopefully the wrinkles would drop out in time. From my coat, I mean, not his hands. There was no remedy for them, and the problem was Anno Domini.

He was weakening. 'You said you'd help.' What hope there was faded from his eyes.

'I offered you money,' I corrected him. 'I'm sorry, really I am, but I can't help you turn back time. Not without calling in many more favours than I currently have saved up.'

'You promised.' He was going for my coat again, but I managed to step aside. 'Yesterday,' he went on. 'You promised yesterday that you'd help.'

'Sweetie – I've never seen you before in my life. Or yours.'

Then he really surprised me. He stuffed his hands into his jacket pockets and pulled out handfuls of money. He had small hands, but they were big handfuls. Ten-dollar bills, crumpled and creased as much as his weather-beaten face. He threw the money at me, right there in the street. It blizzarded round my head, caught in the breeze and swirling through the evening. People stopped and gawped and grabbed.

I just watched. Watched the money spin and fall. Watched the last hope fade from the old man's eyes as his knees buckled and he fell to the sidewalk. Watched his hand flop into the gutter where the rainwater running into a storm drain washed the dust and grime from his cuffs.

Under the layers of age and the wrinkles and pockmarks the man was almost unrecognisable. Almost. But I recognised him now. Just as I recognised the suit he was wearing, the pattern and the colour bright and restored where the water rinsed away the dust and the dirt.

It was the same suit that Rock Railton had been wearing when he called on me yesterday and I promised to help him.

Chapter 3

Lady Don't Shoot

I was wrong of course. It was just some tramp who'd had the good fortune to find a suit from the same store where Rock Railton shopped (OK, one with pockets stuffed with cash, but everyone gets lucky sometimes). An old man who was so confused and so close to death that he thought he knew me, that he would ask a stranger for help. He didn't want to die – well, that's hardly a surprise.

Nothing to see here, move right along, please.

I did the helpless thing again and some of the passers-by stopped jumping for ten-dollar bills long enough to realise the old guy needed some help. Or rather, that he was past it.

'Let me through – I'm a doctor.'

My heart beat a little faster, and I lingered just long enough to be sure he'd used the indefinite article. But the man was short and bald and rather ugly – not at all like any Doctor I'd consult. I hope. If 'consult' is the right word.

By the time I reached Nick's I was completely composed again and ready to perform my renowned raincoat removal routine. I assured myself that the statue still hadn't moved, and then caught sight of Rock Railton walking into Nick's ahead of me. Any final doubts or worries I might have had disappeared as quick as the sun in an English summer.

The doorman frowned at me when I introduced myself. 'Miss Malone – you're not on the list.'

'Maybe not your list, sweetie. But I'm on nearly everyone else's.' It didn't take a lot to persuade him to let me in.

Rock had already disappeared deep into the melee of guests. I did the raincoat thing and draped it over the arm of a nearby waiter, not bothering to check how many people had watched. I recognised the sound of jaws dropping.

The waiter holding my coat, and apparently attempting to make eye contact somewhere south of my own jaw, directed me through the large foyer to the ballroom where the party was being held.

Another waiter appeared beside me before I was three steps into room.

He offered up a silver tray of fluted glasses. 'Champagne?'

'I prefer the real thing,' I assured him in a loud whisper. I took a glass anyway and surveyed the room as I sipped. It wasn't bad. But it wasn't very French either.

My plan, such as it was, centred on talking to

Rock Railton and getting an idea of who the likely suspects were. Chances were that whoever wanted him dead was in this room – and I don't just mean the critics.

Everyone was here. I recognised other movie stars, like Giddy Semestre whose neckline was even more pronounced than my own. It didn't so much plunge as plummet. I spotted some big-name producers including Maximilian Schneider dePost von Algonquin – who has to be one of the biggest names in any industry.

Then there was the press. I knew some of the owners of the big papers very well indeed. They fell into two camps – those who smiled and raised their glasses in greeting when they saw me, and those who turned away and tried to hide their faces in the hope I wouldn't recognise or remember them. I could write a few headlines there.

I couldn't for the moment see Rock Railton, so I made my way across the room towards Giddy Semestre. She was the co-star of *Lady Don't Shoot*, and there were rumours that she and Rock were romantically linked. At the hip. Whatever the truth of that, it seemed likely that Rock would gravitate towards Giddy before too long.

Plus it's always nice to talk to the most beautiful and intelligent woman in the room. So Giddy would be grateful for the opportunity.

I reached Giddy and her entourage in time to hear the end of a rather obvious joke and leaned forward in order to steal the punchline.

There was a moment's silence, into which I added: 'Sorry – were you actually telling the version with the minotaur and the ukulele?' Several people drifted away after that and soon I was alone with Miss Semestre.

'I'm sorry, but have we met before?' she asked.

I shook my head. 'I'm sure you'd remember.'

She smiled, raised a perfectly pencilled eyebrow, and looked me up and down. 'I'm sure I would.'

'I'm a friend of Rock Railton.'

'That may not narrow things down very much,' she said.

'Do I look like I need narrowing down?' I wondered. I congratulated her on her performance in the movie. Her smile widened alarmingly as I poured on the praise for her acting abilities.

But she wasn't as dizzy as her name suggested. It was genuine amusement rather than immodesty. 'You haven't actually seen the movie, have you?' she said.

I had to confess that I'd skipped the movie bit and come straight to the party. 'But I'm sure you were very good in it.'

'You can sure lie,' she said, smile still in place. 'But I can't act to save my life. Oh, I have no illusions about that,' she went on before I could pretend to disagree. 'I'm there to look good. And maybe my looks are the best act of the lot.'

I asked her what she meant. Even up this close she wasn't as heavily made-up as most of the women in the room. I'd passed one lady who had arrived well plastered in every sense.

Before she could answer me, a short man with oiled-back thinning hair who looked like he'd needed some of the same oil to ease him into his bulging suit arrived. He smudged the back of Giddy's hand with his greasy lips.

'Darling!' he announced, as if this was a complete conversation. 'Darrr-ling!' he said again – you could practically hear the subject- verb-object construction within those two syllables.

He straightened up from the kiss, though that didn't buy him much height, and looked at me askance. 'Who's your friend?'

Giddy was giving the lie to her comments about her own acting talents by making a good job of hiding her disgust at the guy's slobbering. 'Oh, Max – this is…' She stumbled.

I helped her out. 'Melody Malone.'

'Melody Malone, eh?' He sounded like he reckoned I'd just made the name up. So maybe he was more perceptive than I thought. 'What studio you with?'

'I'm not in the movie business,' I confessed.

He pursed his lips in an especially unpleasant manner. 'You ever decide you should be, give me a call.' He bowed just enough for me to get the full impact of his bald patch. My guess was he didn't know that from this angle he looked like a monk at prayer.

'And you are?' I asked.

That hit him right between the eyes just as

he straightened up. There was a certain amount of spluttering from the Monk-Man, and barely concealed amusement from Miss Gillespie.

'I'm kidding,' I said in my bestest silkiest voice.

He obviously believed I must indeed be joking, and turned to share the amusement with Giddy, allowing me time to give her an exaggerated blank look.

Luckily she realised I hadn't a clue as to his identity and rescued me. I don't often need rescuing, but it's nice when it goes well and doesn't involve great heights.

'Oh, Miss Malone, you're such a tease,' Giddy said. 'Everyone knows Max Kliener, head of Starlight Studios. He produced *Lady Don't Shoot*, of course.'

'Of course.' Well, yes, I'd heard of Kliener. I always thought he sounded like a commercial for an industrial vacuum appliance, and made a mental note to tell him some time. But maybe not just now.

Kliener jabbed a podgy finger at me several times, while looking me up and down and appraising me in a way that seemed particularly unnecessary. 'Had me there,' he said.

'You wish,' I murmured.

'But, like I said – you decide to get into movies, I can find a place for you at Starlight. Just come down to the set any time and ask for Max Kliener. Everyone knows Max.'

I switched on my own oiliest smile. 'You sure about that... Max – was it?'

He exploded with laughter. Well, not literally

– that might have been more amusing. But it was a pretty extreme reaction, and completely out of proportion to my admittedly witty repost.

I didn't linger. Max Kliener was not the sort of man a woman with any choice would linger with. From the fact that Giddy Semestre did linger, I deduced that she probably didn't have a choice. I'm a detective – I can tell.

Meanwhile, I'd caught sight of Rock Railton on the other side of the room. He was surrounded by several women of an age where their own choices were likely to be severely limited, an insincere smile painted across his face and his moustache twitching in near panic. The poor boy needed help – Melody Malone to the rescue.

He looked relieved, I'll give him that. I was holding out for awestruck, but one step at a time.

'I'm sorry, ladies,' I announced in my huskiest and most urgent tone. 'But I'm going to have to steal Mr Railton away for a few moments. Work as well as pleasure today.'

I left it to them to guess which of the two this might be. From some of the looks I got, a few of them guessed correctly.

'I guess I owe you a thank you,' Railton said as we moved off into the crowd.

'I guess you do.'

He nodded and smiled as we moved through the great and the good. Or at least, the rich and the famous which, as you can imagine, is not always the same thing. In this case a two-circled Venn Diagram would have had precious little by way of intersection.

We reached a secluded corner, and he smiled. 'Will you at least tell me your name?' I probably didn't hide my surprise as well as I usually do, because he quickly went on: 'I'm sorry if we've met before. I meet so many people.'

Over his shoulder, I could see Max Kliener staring nervously in our direction. He excused himself from the group he was with and headed over.

'You really don't remember me?' I nodded, understanding. Composure level set to iceberg. 'Melody Malone. Well, I suppose it's been a while.'

'I suppose it has.' He pointed at me, the way people do when they want you to think they've realised or remembered something. 'Must be – how long?'

'Oh, don't be coy. I think you remember exactly when we last met, Mr Railton.' I adjusted his necktie for him, and stepped back to admire my handiwork.

Kliener had been accosted on the way over by a large gentleman I didn't yet know was Julius Grayle. Corpulent, ageing and corrupt – though I knew only two of those for certain back then, of course. He was gesturing emphatically, while Kliener sneaked furtive and worried glances at me and Rock.

'Yes,' Rock Railton was saying, 'Melody Malone. We met at…'

I didn't help him, just tilted my head winningly and smiled some more.

'…at that *thing*. Must be six, seven…'

Still no help. I raised an eyebrow.

'Possibly as much as…' he went on.

I put him out of his misery. 'We met at my office. Yesterday afternoon.'

He went white. Not out of embarrassment – he really did not know who I was, and my words had genuinely shocked him.

I collected a glass of 'champagne' from a passing tray attached to a waiter and took a sip. It was unpleasantly warm.

'But I can understand that it's slipped your memory,' I said in my most understanding tone. 'After all, we only flirted outrageously.'

He nodded, as if that was to be expected.

'I'm a detective, as you perhaps recall. And you told me someone was going to kill you. Ringing any bells yet?'

I didn't think it was possible for him to go any paler. But he did. He swallowed, and took a step backwards, clumsily knocking into a waiter – who immediately apologised.

'You'll have to excuse me,' he stammered. 'I've… I've just seen someone I recognise.'

He hurried away, almost taking out another waiter, two women, and the human bowling-ball that was Max Kliener in his haste.

'Must be someone you've known for less than twelve hours then,' I murmured.

Chapter 4
Death and Taxis

I'd had enough of taxis for the moment, and even in New York the air is fresh enough to clear the head. A brisk walk across town might not be the best prescription for every woman heading home alone. But then I'm not every woman.

New York can be a dangerous place. Even in my grey raincoat I seemed to attract attention. Maybe it was the heels. Or perhaps the fedora.

Whatever the attraction, I was soon aware of two men following me. They kept to the shadows, which from the rare glimpses I caught of their faces was probably just as well for everyone.

A shadow flitting across a puddle. A distorted reflection in a store window. The fact that neither of them seemed capable of walking without their boot nails clicking on the sidewalk. It all added up to mischief, with me as the target. I like to know where I am with people. Especially people with guns.

There's a narrow, badly lit passageway that cuts through from Kemmerton to Flale Street. No one in their right mind would ever use it after dark. I waited until I was halfway along it, then stepped into a doorway. It was the back door of a laundry. If you didn't know it was there you'd never spot it in a hundred years. And I was planning on being away long before the hundred years was up.

The two guys were clever enough to know this was an opportunity. Not clever enough to realise *whose* opportunity, but it still put them pretty high on the thug-ometer.

To give them due credit, they didn't take long to work out I'd disappeared. Well, I guess it's not that hard to discern in a sort of 'now you see me, now you – where the hell?' sort of way. They stopped, turned, looked at each other, frowned. All while standing under the only lamp in the alley, so I had a clear view of them. A clear shot too, except I didn't have a gun. They did – one each in fact. But I tend to think it's not polite to pack artillery at a swanky party. Cleavage, but not shooters.

Having stood in a clear line of sight under a lamp, waving pistols and making woefully inarticulate 'Er – what?' noises to each other, the two thugs then did something really stupid.

They split up. One headed back up the alley and the other continued down it, leaving me alone in the middle. Not very helpful. I sighed and stepped out of the doorway.

'Hello, boys. You looking for me?'

They both turned at once.

'I noticed you were following me a while back.'

They approached warily, guns raised.

'It's the heels, isn't it?' I looked from one to the other. 'Be honest. The heels. Or is it the hat? I rather like the hat.' I adjusted the brim, making one of them jab his gun forwards – like I was going to kill him with my hat. Well, I've done that before actually, so maybe he wasn't so daft.

'Not very talkative, are we?' I went on. They were standing either side of me now, each about ten feet away. 'If fashion isn't your strong suit, then let's try an easier one. Who sent you?'

'You're the Melody Malone dame,' one of them growled.

It was tempting to say 'no' and see how they reacted. They might just apologise and walk away. Or they might shoot me anyway. So instead I smiled and asked:

'What if I am?'

'We gotta kill you,' the other thug said. As I turned to look at him he shrugged and added, 'Sorry, lady.' Well, it was a step up from 'dame'.

'It's me who should apologise.' I unbuttoned my raincoat and they gripped their guns all the tighter.

Neither of them got any more talkative, and the contents of their pockets didn't help much either. I dropped their guns in a trash can outside the back of the laundry, and left their wallets on the wet cobbles beside them.

I helped myself to a few dollars from one wallet for a taxi back to the office. Expenses. I imagined he'd have other things to worry about when he woke up.

'It's definitely the heels,' I told them as I walked away.

The cab driver was less talkative than his predecessor, which suited me fine. He dropped me outside the office and disappeared into the night at a restrained pace and without need of his horn. But with a healthy tip thanks to the generous gentleman with the gun, the wallet, and (by now) the headache.

I sat with my feet up on my desk and started to make a mental list of the people who'd want me dead. Once I got to fifty, I decided this wasn't helping. I narrowed the criteria to people in New York, in 1938, and finally who I'd met in the last month. It gave me a more manageable number and a few smiles. But it didn't really help much.

So I decided to concentrate on the last couple of days. Maybe one of the women I'd deprived of the company of Rock Railton? Murder did seem a little extreme but it was a possibility. Someone I'd upstaged with my stun-level-five outfit? Well that could be any of the female guests at the party, and possibly a few of the male ones.

Most likely it was connected to the Rock Railton case. I'm a big fan of coincidence, but even so if someone tells you their life is in danger and the next day a couple of thugs come gunning for you, then there is at least the possibility of a connection.

Which got me thinking about Rock himself, and

how bizarre his behaviour had been. I flatter myself
that I'm at least a little distinctive in both character
and – let's face it – looks. I make an impression.
People don't forget me in a hurry.

Yet Rock Railton had dismissed me from his mind
by the next day. That isn't the way to flatter a girl.
Unless it was an act, of course. And unlike a lot of
the Starlight Stars, Railton *could* act.

Soon I had a working theory. Railton had
pretended he didn't know me because he was aware
that whoever was trying to kill him could come after
me if they were aware I was on the case.

'You sweetie,' I breathed. He only had my safety
in mind. That had to be it.

In fact, I could not have been more wrong. But
hindsight is a wonderful thing and – for most people
– only comes after the event.

The result was that I was in a less thoughtful
mood when the telephone rang. I don't get a lot of
calls, so I enjoyed the novelty of the noise for a while
before I answered.

'Hello, Angel,' I said, which usually throws them.
But not in this case.

'Hello, doll.'

I paused to stare at the receiver like it was to blame.
But it was my fault for answering. I recognised his
voice, and now I had to speak to him.

'Mr Kliener,' I enthused. 'How clever of you to
ring my bell.'

He laughed his oily laugh. 'Didn't know you
were a tec.'

'I am so many things.'

'Wasn't easy, as I only had your name.'

'Really?' I inspected my nails, and was not surprised to find them perfect in every detail.

'No one seemed to know how to get hold of you.'

'The right person starts by buying me a drink.'

He didn't react to that. I guess it was a bit over his head, which given his stature wouldn't be hard.

'How *did* you track me down?' I asked as the silence stretched out. Really, I just preferred the sound of my own voice to the sound of his.

'You won't believe this, but I asked a guy called Garner. He's done some work for Julius Grayle – you know him?'

'I know Garner slightly,' I told him. 'He's in the same business I am.'

'Yeah, I know that now.'

So Max Kliener had hired a private detective to find another private detective. It's a pity the Americans don't really understand irony.

'So how can I help you, Mr Kliener?'

'Please – call me Max,' he oiled.

'Fine.' That was easy. 'Anything else, Max?'

Unfortunately there was. But as it was an invitation to come down to the Starlight Studios complex, it might help me move forward with the Rock Railton case.

'Rock and Giddy should be in full flow this afternoon starting on their new picture. I'll arrange a car for you.'

'Personal taxi service, I'm impressed.'

'Least I can do.'

I wasn't sure why he felt he had to spend time and money on my account. Except, of course, that he'd met me.

'Well,' I told him, 'I suppose that in this life there's nothing that can be said to be certain except death and taxis.'

He didn't comment. So I assumed he wasn't a big devotee of Benjamin Franklin, and listed that alongside Max Kliener's other failings. It was getting to be quite a list.

But I still agreed to see him at the studio that afternoon. It seemed like a good move. But like I said, for most people hindsight only works backwards.

Chapter 5
Lights, Camera, Bizarre

Back then, all cars were black. But some were more black than others. The car Max Kliener sent to collect me that afternoon was so black that light seemed to slide off it. The driver wore a dark uniform that looked pale in comparison. He introduced himself as Hank. I could believe that – he looked like a Hank.

He was about six foot six in height, and as wide as he was tall. Not *bad* wide, just *wide* wide. I suspected his uniform had been put together from at least two other normal-sized suits. He had strikingly blond hair that contrasted with dark eyes and a nose that in the past had seen both better days and – I would bet good money – the wrong end of a large fist. I would have asked him about that, but he wasn't a great conversationalist. What he did say sounded like it had been filtered through gravel.

The result of which was that the journey to Starlight Studios was conducted in near silence. With the dark-tinted windows and an opaque partition obscuring the driver, I felt like I was being wheeled along in an isolation tank completely cut off from the real world. But New York's a bit like that anyway.

The ride was so smooth I didn't realise we'd stopped until Hank opened the door to let me out. I was glad of my dark glasses as the sun was angling in over the long, low sheds that were the film studios. Hank had parked the car outside one of them, and Max Kliener was standing nearby talking to a lean man with a clipboard. He had a cigar clamped in his mouth, though it didn't seem to be lit. He removed it to gesture and prod the air, like it was a prop.

When he saw me, Kliener opened his arms and waddled forwards. I avoided an embrace and shook his hand instead. It was cold and clammy and damp, like shaking a fish that's been dead for a couple of days. If you know what that feels like.

'Melody Melody Melody,' Kliener enthused. He stepped back to look me up and down. I'm used to being looked up and down but it was still a bit disconcerting. Like meeting your own undertaker for the first time.

'Max Max Max,' I reciprocated. 'How kind of you to invite me to your quaint little place.'

His mouth smiled to show he took it as a joke. His eyes hadn't quite got the message and glared angrily.

Hank stayed with us as Max led me through a side door into the studio. Inside was bigger than an aircraft hangar and hotter than a sauna because of all the lights.

The lion's share of the lighting was reserved for the set where they were shooting. It was a ballroom furnished in the style of Renaissance Italy. I refrained from pointing out a few obvious mistakes. I doubt if accuracy was foremost in the mind of the designer or the costume department. It was a little strange seeing the room only half built – with walls omitted to allow the cameramen access. But I can cope with 'strange'. It's only when we get to 'bizarre' that I start to get tingly.

We watched Rock and Giddy rehearse their scene in front of the cameras. The director – all shirtsleeves and megaphone – interrupting every few minutes. It was like both of the stars were novices, having to be told what to do every step of the way. That might have intrigued me, if I hadn't had Max Kliener whispering obvious explanations uncomfortably close to my ear. The main distraction was that he had to stand on tiptoe to do it.

As the cast took a break to set up the lights and cameras ready for the next shot, Kliener gestured to Rock Railton, beckoning him over. A make-up woman moved in quickly on Giddy Semestre – all powder puff and potions. She had the sort of severe features and iron-grey hair that would scare anyone into looking their best.

'He wants to apologise,' Kliener told me as Rock negotiated a path through cables and technicians. 'Dunno what got into him last night. Making like he didn't know you and all that.'

I said nothing. How did Kliener know what had

happened? Railton must have told him – but why?
That didn't fit with my working hypothesis. Time
for a new theory, perhaps.

'He's very highly strung,' Kliener added in a low
voice as Rock joined us. 'Problems with his meds.'

Rock greeted me like a long-lost friend, pulling
me into a bear hug that more than made up for the
previous evening. If he'd been a really good actor, I
might have been convinced. But while there was no
doubt he *could* act, he was competent, little more.

So when he apologised for forgetting we'd met
before the party and that he'd actually been to my
offices, I smiled my forgiveness.

'It's been such a hectic schedule,' he said. 'So
much going on. I don't know what I was thinking –
didn't know if I was coming or going.'

'That can be such a problem,' I agreed. 'Just so
long as you remember me now.'

'How could I forget you, Miss Malone?'

'Well, quite.' Railton and Kliener were smiling
so hard it seemed a shame to puncture the moment.
But if anyone is completely without shame, then I'm
not ashamed to say it's me. 'And my coffee,' I said.

'Your… coffee?'

'Best coffee you'd ever tasted, you told me. I'm
sure you remember that. You asked whether I grind
my own beans.'

His eyes widened slightly and his moustache
twitched. 'It *was* the best coffee I've ever tasted,' he
assured me. 'Unique.'

'You're too kind,' I told him. Which he was – far

too kind. Because now I knew he was lying. OK, so maybe it was a failing on my part, but I didn't even offer him coffee.

Even so we were still in the territory marked as 'Strange' or possibly 'Weird'. But 'Bizarre' was just around the corner.

It arrived in the form of Giddy Semestre. She walked up to Rock and Kliener, working her hips so hard she swayed through about twice the distance she needed to travel. She put her hand on Rock's shoulder, leaning slightly towards me. Somehow she seemed rather less confident and more 'dizzy' than she had the night before. Still, at least I could be sure she would remember me.

'So, Rocky,' she breathed, nodding at me. 'Who's your glamorous lady friend?'

It was like she'd never met me before – and not just because she used the term 'lady'.

I needed some time to think about this, and maybe come up with another theory that could later prove to be completely wrong. So I accepted Kliener's offer of a tour of the rest of the studio complex.

My brain was working so hard that I barely took in the details. Kliener's voice was an unguent drone. One vast studio looked much like another, even with sets being built or dismantled. I confess I paid more attention when we got to the costume department. I passed a pleasant few minutes examining Giddy Semestre's cast-offs, which hung in a wardrobe running the length of the back wall.

'I guess you're about the same height,' Kliener said, wiping his forehead with a sweat-stained handkerchief.

'I guess we are.' It wasn't something I'd considered.

'About the same size too. So what do you weigh?' He made a guess that was slightly on the generous side. Whether that was generous to me or to the weight, I'll leave to your imagination.

But I told Kliener: 'I never discuss my weight before the third cocktail.'

'Maybe I can do something about that,' he smarmed.

Maybe not, I thought. I was beginning to get concerned at the lack of clues in this case. Possibly a lack of client too, as Rock Railton evidently had no real recollection of hiring me. Or presumably agreeing my fee.

Perhaps my impatience was showing, because Kliener assured me there was just one more stop on the tour. Just one more thing he wanted me to see. 'It'll blow you away,' he promised.

Well, we live in hope.

Hank was waiting outside the costume store. For some reason he'd ditched the dark (but not that dark) suit in favour of light tan trousers and a blazer. He cracked his knuckles alarmingly as we emerged and he became our shadow as Kliener led the way down an alley that ran alongside the building.

Our destination was a nondescript block away from the main complex. It looked insignificant in the way that only something that is supposed to remain unremarked can. The bolts and locks on the door were shiny from frequent use, but there was no sign of another living soul.

Inside was dark. Kliener fumbled for a light switch while Hank pulled the door shut behind us.

'You considered a life in the movies, Miss Malone?' Kliener said as the lights snapped on.

'I think you asked me that before.'

'Maybe I did. But your height and weight...'

'What about them?'

Lights were flickering into luminescence all around. The whole building was one vast chamber, like the studios. Except this obviously wasn't a studio.

'I reckon you'd make a good double for Giddy Semestre.'

He had to be joking. Giddy's figure, while perfect in its own way, was rather different from my own just-as-perfect figure. Sure, we both had curves in the same places. But not always in exactly the same direction or at the same angle. There were bits of Giddy Semestre that entered a room long before the rest of her, and believe me that would be a distinct disadvantage for a private detective who prides herself on being able to sneak into rooms all at roughly the same time.

But whatever witty retort I might have made was stifled by the sight of the inside of the building as the lights came on. The centre of the chamber was taken up with a large coffin-shaped tank. Pipes and tubes and cables and wires fed into and out of it, running to various pieces of advanced – for 1938 – equipment. More wires and cables emerged from the equipment and disappeared behind a heavy curtain close to one of the walls.

Stretching out beyond the tank were several rows of what looked like glass bell jars. Except they were enormous – maybe ten feet high.

I'd never seen anything like it. And things I've never seen anything like worry me. Because I have seen so many things. What surprises life has left for me tend, for some reason, to be unpleasant ones.

Instead of wasting my wit, therefore, I decided it was time to be on my way.

Hank was standing with Kliener off to one side, so my route back to the door was clear. Never one to miss an opportunity or inspect the teeth of a horse someone's donated, I made my way rapidly back to the door and flung it open.

Only to find Hank standing on the other side. He cracked his knuckles and smiled. One of these actions made a noise like a gunshot. I had a horrible feeling it was the smile.

The obvious conclusion that any half-decent detective might come to at this stage, confronted with a Hank in the doorway and aware of another identical Hank standing behind her is that they were twins. One in a dark suit, the other in slacks and a blazer. I discarded this conclusion at once.

Partly this was because when I turned back to face Kliener and slacks-Hank, I saw that a *third* Hank was approaching across the chamber.

Mostly it was because as more lights flickered into life on the far side of the coffin-shaped tank, I could see what was inside the bell jars.

Leaning against the glass, for all the world like propped-up mannequins, were people. One in each jar. A whole line of identical Rock Railtons stood facing a whole line of identical Giddy Semestres.

'Here's the thing,' I said to the Hank who had just grabbed my arms from behind and was holding me more tightly than a nervous bridegroom. 'I may be wrong about this, but I'm willing to go out on a limb at least until you tear my limbs out. And I am guessing that you do not come from a family of identical triplets.'

Chapter 6

The Soul of Wit

I was allowed to walk back unaided to where Max Kliener was waiting. But two Hanks followed closely behind me, each holding an identical pistol in their identical hands. Max Kliener, meanwhile, had transformed into Max Show-off.

He seemed only slightly put out when I interrupted his spiel to say: 'It was you that sent those thugs to kill me last night after the party, wasn't it?'

He opened his hands in a 'what can I say' gesture. 'After Rock told me he should have recognised you and didn't, I was worried how much you knew.'

'Which Rock was that?' I asked, pleased I'd timed my question to coincide with walking past several of them propped up inside their bell jars. We really were in the country of the bizarre now.

'It's best to plan ahead,' Kliener told me. 'You never know when you might need a new star.'

'So the first Rock was right when he said someone

was out to kill him.'

Kliener shook his head. 'Wrong on every count, lady.' He was starting to annoy me.

But I smiled to show otherwise. 'Oh?'

'He wasn't the first Rock, not by a long way. And no one was trying to kill him. It just… happens.'

Light was beginning to dawn. I could understand the attraction of having a ready supply of the world's best-known movie stars standing by. If they were in the habit of dying off, that made even more sense.

But where did Kliener get them from? I glanced back at the coffin-shaped tank and he clapped his hands approvingly.

'I think the dame's got it,' he said. 'Clever girl.'

'Lady, dame, girl, make your mind up.' All right, so my mind was on working out the plot rather than witty dialogue right now. 'You have a way of making someone look how you want – am I right?'

'Top of the class, doll.'

'You asked about my height and weight, so I'm guessing it's to do with moving bits round rather than hacking them about.' I had a vague idea of how it might work, but he'd need the sort of power supply that wasn't readily available in 1930s New York.

'That's right.' Kliener took his cigar out of his mouth for long enough to examine it and seem surprised it wasn't lit. 'It's all to do with redistribution of flesh and bone matter.' He knocked on the nearest bell jar and it made a dull ringing sound. 'These are all different people. But now, thanks to my work, they look the same.'

'But they're asleep,' I pointed out. 'They're even more bored with what you've done than I am.'

He chomped his cigar. 'Funny girl. They're just waiting till I need them. As you know I got a costume store, and a prop store and a scenery store. Now I got a star store too.'

I peered through the glass at a sleeping Giddy Semestre. She looked just like the real thing. Though, I realised, I'd probably never met the real thing. I wondered who she used to be.

'What happens to them?' I was asking myself as much as Kliener. My breath misted the glass as I spoke, blurring the woman's sleeping features.

'They die.' He said it easily, like it was no big deal. Like it wasn't the most important event in his star's short life. 'The process doesn't last. A couple of weeks, then they pay the price for being beautiful. I guess you burn too bright you don't burn for long.'

'They get old,' I realised. I remembered the old tramp outside Nick's when I was on my way to the launch party. That had been the Rock Railton I met the day before – the one I had promised to help. Too late for him now.

'They just sort of crumble away,' Kliener said. 'Sad. But, hey, that's life. Or rather...' He paused to guffaw unpleasantly. It was the sort of sound a donkey might make if it was in intense pain and beyond embarrassment. 'Or rather – that's *death*.'

I didn't share his amusement. 'So they die, and you just wheel out a new version. An identical copy.'

'You got it. Have to animate them first – wake

them up. Then the clock starts ticking. Two weeks they got, if they're lucky. That's why I keep a few spares. I find a suitable candidate, and I process them ready for when I need them. A word to the press that they've set their sights on Hollywood and no one's the wiser.'

'But what,' I asked as sweetly as I could stomach, 'if they don't want to cooperate? It might be news to you, but not everyone in this world wants to be a famous movie star.'

'That's no problem. They forget. They forget everything when they wake up. They think they really *are* Rock Railton or Giddy Semestre.'

'Or Hank?'

Kliener's eyes narrowed and his cigar drooped slightly. 'Or Hank,' he agreed.

'You have a template,' I guessed. 'They only have the memories the real person had at the point that was made. Which is why a new Rock Railton doesn't know what the last one got up to or who he met. Same with Giddy Semestre. Same with Hank.'

His eyes had narrowed so far now that they were in danger of disappearing altogether. He knew it was coming, so before he could work out what to do about it, I turned to face the two Hanks with guns.

'So how long have these guys got?' I asked. 'Before they "just sort of crumble away"?'

Neither Hank showed any sign of understanding the point I was trying to make. Kliener had obviously chosen their template for physical rather than mental acuity. I glanced back at the third Hank who was making some adjustments to the coffin-tank. I doubted he knew what 'acuity' meant either.

Beyond him, a fourth Hank had appeared in the doorway. He was escorting the severe-looking middle-aged make-up woman I'd seen in the studio. From her expression I reckoned I'd rather let Lizzie Borden work on my looks than this hatchet-faced harridan.

Between them, the new Hank and hatchet-face were supporting another woman. It took me a moment to recognise Giddy Semestre. As they approached, I heard Kliener gasp beside me. It wasn't hard to tell why.

Giddy's face was drawn and her hair was turning grey. Her forehead was lined, and crow's feet framed her eyes. She looked like she had aged twenty years since I last saw her about an hour earlier.

'Already?' Kliener said.

'It's getting quicker,' Harridan-Woman said. 'We need another one quick – they're still shooting.'

Giddy looked up at me, confused and afraid. Maybe she recognised me as the one person here who might have some sympathy. Well, she was right there.

'What's happening to me?' she asked in a throaty rasp. Her face looked even more wrinkled than it had just moments before.

'Nothing to worry about, doll,' Kliener said. 'The show must go on.'

And with that he stepped forward, drew a pistol from inside his jacket pocket, and shot her clean through the head.

I say 'clean'. In fact, it was anything but. It would take Make-Up Lady a few minutes to sort out herself and Fourth-Hank.

The bloodstains also spattered the curtain that partitioned off a small area off to the side of the equipment attached to the coffin-tank. I'd noted the cables and wires snaking underneath the curtain earlier. Well hey – I'm a detective. I notice things. And the thing I noticed now was that the curtain shimmered, as if in a breeze. From behind it came a noise that was partway between a sigh and a sharp intake of breath.

If Kliener noticed, he didn't show it. 'Less than two days this time.' He sounded worried – and it wasn't the sort of concern one might naturally expect to feel after shooting dead one of the world's most famous women.

He knelt beside Giddy's body, which was lying face down. He turned her over. There was a neat hole drilled through her wrinkled forehead and she looked, well let's face it – dead.

As we watched, the wrinkles deepened, the flesh sagged, the skin became translucent. Impossibly, she was still ageing. I tried to calculate how fast I could get to Kliener without being shot by a Hank. It didn't take me long to decide it was impossible. And in that same short time, the late Giddy Semestre – or whoever she had really been – crumbled to dust. A few moments later, and all that was left was a faint outline on the floor. Even the blood had flaked away, disintegrating to leave only a vague stain.

No one else seemed the least bit surprised or shocked by all this. I gave up on surprise a long time ago, and I'm not easily shocked. But Kliener's casual viciousness appalled me. With two of the Hanks still covering me with their guns, and another two busy nearby, there was nothing I could do. Not yet.

Besides, I have to confess I was curious to see what happened next. Everything about me is pretty and a lot of it is shrewd. So I had a pretty shrewd idea what was going on.

The two spare Hanks – by which I mean the ones who were not busily watching me and waiting for an excuse to shoot – moved to the nearest bell jar. Inside, a sleeping Giddy Semestre leaned against the glass. She was wearing a plain white dress, her features every bit as young and beautiful as in the film posters. Or as I had seen her at the party and then again on set.

One of the Hanks produced a large axe. The other Hank, Kliener and Mrs Make-Up stood well clear as Axe-Hank swung at the bell jar. The glass exploded, showering down on Hank. He seemed as oblivious to it as he probably was to the meaning of the word. Giddy slopped out, one slender arm thrown forward, a shapely leg visible where her dress had got hitched up. No one seemed worried she might get cut on the glass. Someone was going to have some sweeping up to do. Big time.

Hank and Hank lifted Giddy with surprising delicacy. They carried her over to Kliener, standing her on her feet. She swayed like a sleepwalker, and Kliener supported her – head lolling on his shoulder, his arm round her. With a helping hand from the make-up harridan, he walked Giddy across to the curtain.

The make-up woman pulled the curtain open just far enough for me not to be able to see behind it, but sufficient for Kliener and Giddy to pass through.

A few moments later, they were back. Giddy was still relying on Kliener for support, but now she was awake. She looked disoriented and confused. She looked a little, well, giddy.

She saw me, she saw the Hanks, she seemed to recognise none of us. Only Kliener and the make-up woman – the only people the real Giddy Semestre had known when she was 'templated'.

'Giddy!' I called out. I got a pistol jabbed in my midriff for my pains. It didn't shut me up. 'They're using you, Giddy. Don't believe a thing they tell you. Don't even believe who you are. Try to remember who you used to be, who you really were!'

The gun jabbed harder, and I shut up. Not because of the gun, but because from her expression Giddy obviously thought I was mad.

'I'm sorry,' she said, shaking her head sadly. 'I'm due on set and I have lines to learn. It will take me a while.'

'Way things are going,' I said to her back as she left, 'it could take you a lifetime.'

I turned to Kliener who was watching his latest protégé leave. He looked about ready to bite the end off his cigar, he was so pleased with himself.

'You said yourself, it's accelerating,' I reminded him. 'How long does *she* have, do you suppose? A whole day if she's lucky? A couple of hours, maybe?'

Kliener's smile might have been pasted on his face for all the change there was in his expression. He walked slowly up to me.

'I'd better make sure I have her replacement lined up, then.' He nodded at the line of Giddy bell jars. 'As many replacements as I can find.'

'You're insane,' I told him.

I don't think he was even listening. His face was looking as pleased as punch – which was what I was going to do to it just as soon as I got the chance. Cigar and all.

Kliener leaned towards me, even though the top of his head was roughly level with my shoulder. 'Bet you're wondering how all this is possible,' he smarmed.

It was a shame to puncture the moment. Actually, that's a bit of a lie. I enjoyed looking him in the top of the head and sighing patiently as if I was explaining things simply to a rather dim-witted child.

'Not at all,' I said. 'You obviously have an Angel.'

Chapter 7
The Stone Cold Killer

I got ample confirmation of Kliener's complete indifference to irony: when I mentioned the Angel, he looked up at me sharply – and *blinked*. Then, in case I hadn't found that amusing and ironic enough, he did it some more. There was a nervous tick at the side of his eye too. I suspected he wasn't especially delighted at the way I'd stolen his thunder. I was unrepentant – I think he'd stolen more than that in his time.

And thinking of time brought me back to the Angel, which I now knew from his reaction Kliener had hidden behind the curtain. Where no one could see it. God knows what it was doing – out of sight but not out of mind.

'Where's this going to end?' I demanded while Kliener was failing to come up with a response. 'Can't you see what's happening? The process is speeding up. It's taking more energy as it gets stronger. And the stronger the Angel gets the more energy it takes which accelerates things still further. How long before she's strong enough to escape?'

'You know nothing,' Kliener spat. And I use the word accurately.

'I know more than you,' I told him as I dabbed at my face with a hanky. However apparently tight and uncompromising one's outfit always make sure you have a special handy space for a hanky. And lipstick.

'So what if you do?'

'Well, if I know more than you and I know nothing, then I suppose you know less than nothing. Is that right?'

He didn't seem very interested in the mathematics of it. Instead he wobbled over to the curtain and yanked it aside.

I think even Kliener was surprised by what he revealed. The Angel was leaning forward, its chipped wings swept back as if it was moving at incredible speed. Its gnarled, clawed hands stretched out in front like the talons of an eagle reaching for its prey. The stone face was weathered and lined, but twisted into a hideous snarl of anger, rage, and hunger.

'I am guessing,' I said in my best told-you-so voice, 'that it's repairing itself. That's what it does with all the energy – the potential life it rips away from your victims. And I do mean victims.'

'Not another word out of you, Miss Blabbermouth,' Kliener snapped.

I ignored this skilful quip. 'It uses a fraction of

that energy to shape the next Rock Railton or Giddy Semestre or Hank...' I paused, momentarily thrown. 'What's your last name?' I asked the nearest Hank.

'Sissy,' he said.

'It was a fair question.'

'Hank Sissy,' the other gun-toting Hank said.

'Seriously?'

'No – Sissy.'

Time to move on. 'Rock Railton, Giddy Semestre or Hank Sissy – it uses a fraction of the energy used to remould your victims to take on the memories and appearance of their templates. The rest of the life force it keeps, the rest of the unholy bargain it does with Time, goes to repairing itself. As you can see.'

Well, Kliener was looking, but he probably couldn't see the truth. He didn't want to. He had other things on his mind. In any case it was clear that Max Kliener and the truth had a rather arm's length relationship.

I tried a different tack. 'So how does the Angel wake your sleeping beauties?'

His smile was back, curled round his cigar. 'How else? With a kiss.'

'The kiss of an Angel?'

'The merest touch will do it. But let's call it a kiss. That seems appropriate.'

It would certainly work, and it did seem horribly appropriate. Horrible because it still looked like I was in line for the lips-of-death treatment myself.

This was rather confirmed as Kliener ordered the

two armed Hanks to take me to the coffin-shaped device. The other two Hanks lifted the lid to reveal the dark interior. It looked worryingly like a coffin inside as well.

Sure enough, the two armed Hanks tucked their pistols away inside their jacket-stroke-blazer and each grabbed one of my arms. I was lifted from the ground and marched across to the tank, which was bad news for me.

The bad news for them was that, with my feet now off the ground, I could twist my legs enough to kick out. In a dazzlingly elegant display of athletic symmetry, I inserted one high heel into the most tender area within reach on each of my escorts. They both yelled and doubled over and each let go of me at the same moment, evidently having a similar interest in the symmetry of things.

All of which left me free to get my high heels back under the rest of me and make a rapid exit. My feet clacked on the hard floor like a frantic telegraph operator. SOS all the way to the door.

The door sprang open before I got there. Not good news. It was Mrs Make-Up returning. I caught a satisfying glimpse of her surprised face before I cannoned into it and sent her flying. Unfortunately, the impact sent me flying too.

By the time I got to my feet, I was surrounded by Hank. Just the one Hank, but he held me tight. Then another one jabbed a gun so close to my nose I could smell the cordite from its last shot. If I wasn't careful, my final sensory experience would be the smell of the next one.

Without many options left, I allowed myself to be dragged back towards the coffin-tank. The Make-Up Woman seemed to have recovered from her ordeal, and was talking urgently to Max Kliener.

'Julius can't have it,' Kliener growled. 'Tell him to stop bothering me.' He waved her away.

The woman scowled at me as she passed. I nodded back. But my blood froze as we approached the equipment. The Angel was still staring out from its alcove. Maybe it was a trick of the light, or maybe it was my imagination. But it seemed like the Angel's expression had changed, just slightly.

It seemed like there was the ghost of a smile on its cracked stone lips.

Chapter 8
Angel Kisses

The two Hanks dragged me to the coffin-tank and waited while Max Kliener stomped over. His grin was so wide it looked like his face had split open, probably to let his brain out before there was a major overload.

He stood in front of me and looked me up and down. Mostly up, him being so short. He gestured with his cigar in nothing like the emphatic and effective way that Winston Churchill would soon make famous.

'So, Miss Malone, no final words of regret? No pleading for your life?'

'I'm not intending to die,' I pointed out.

'Don't mean it ain't gonna happen.'

'If I get a last request,' I told him, 'it's that you learn to speak proper English.'

I don't think he really took this to heart as he responded with: 'You want a last request, you got it.

Within reason.'

On the evidence so far, he wouldn't know reason if it came up to him wearing a big badge marked 'Reason', shook hands, and introduced itself. But rather than risk his wrath, or worse his mirth, with a request to leave and go home I asked:

'May I have a minute to compose myself before this ordeal?'

'No problem. But it ain't an ordeal. Soon you'll be the most beautiful woman in the world.'

'That *is* a matter of opinion,' I said. 'And I've a feeling that sort of beauty fades. Fast.'

He nodded, clamping the cigar back in his mouth. 'So compose yourself,' he said rather indistinctly round it. 'You need Hilda to come back and give you the once-over?'

Hilda, I assumed was the hag with the make-up. The notion of her 'giving me the once-over' was almost as unsettling as the prospect of having my flesh and bone re-arranged and then getting snogged by a stone-cold killer. So I declined his thoughtful invitation.

Instead I whipped out my lipstick. One of the Hanks reached for his gun, then realised that I wasn't actually brandishing a weapon. Well – it depends on your definition, I guess.

'There is one other thing,' I said sweetly, noting carefully where each of the four Hanks was positioned. One either side of me, one at the equipment, the last away by the door.

'Shoot.'

I wish, I thought. Though what I actually said was: 'You know, I've always admired you, Max.' Sometimes I surprise myself. 'You've been a hero of mine for so long now.' Remember what I said about shameless. I was laying it on thick, just like the lipstick.

It certainly got his attention. He frowned for a brief moment, but then his vanity got the better of whatever common sense he had. It was obvious that he believed me and was soon lapping it up.

'Go on,' he said.

'No, really. It's a shame about the ageing thing, but even so... The chance to be a genuine Starlight Studios Starlet. Even for just a few days.' My eyelids were fluttering like the wings of a trapped wasp. If he had an ounce of sense he'd realise they were about as safe and friendly.

'My pleasure.' He sounded like he might mean it.

'If only things had worked out differently. But I understand, honestly I do. It's all about protecting your investment, isn't it? I mean, you can't have any old Thomasina, Nicky or Harriet knowing what goes on here, how you've built your success. No matter how clever you've been.'

He made an 'it was nothing' gesture with his cigar which positively dripped with immodesty.

'So I only have one request really,' I told him. 'Because I'm going to forget, aren't I?' I paused to sniff, and then dab a tear from the corner of my eye. 'I'll be such a star. I'll be Giddy Semestre. But me – the real me, *this* me... I'll never know about it.'

He was all sympathy and 'there-there'. Even the Hanks were looking a little moved as I sniffed some more and a real tear rolled down my cheek. Well, *I* was impressed.

'But you know,' I said through my sobs. 'You know, that's all right. That's absolutely fine.'

I turned away so they wouldn't see me crying. Or rather, so they wouldn't see me give in to the urge to roll my eyes and take a deep breath. When I turned back, it looked like I had managed to compose myself again.

'Maybe there's some other way, boss,' one of the Hanks said. I was more disturbed than I expected to see that there was a tear in the corner of his eye too.

'Perhaps it's not too late,' the other Hank agreed.

Well, excuse me – this was my show. My limelight moment. I wanted to look back on this and be able to say: 'All my own work', thank you very much.

I shook my head and waved away their sympathy. 'No, it has to be. I can see that. What choice does poor Mr Kliener – poor *Max* – what choice does he have?'

Maybe I was overdoing it just a touch. Go too far and I'd lose credibility. Now was the moment, so I flung my arms out wide. 'Max – my hero!'

He took a step backwards.

'There is only one thing I want before...' I choked back a sob. 'Before it happens.'

I ran a critical eye over his jacket, then moved as fast as lightning. Before either of the closest Hanks or Max Kliener himself could react, I grabbed him and pulled him into an embrace. Then I kissed him long and hard, full on the lips.

To give him his due, he went with it. I had trouble pulling away. But as soon as I did, he was out of it for a while – my lipstick has that effect.

As Max was coming to terms with having been snogged out of his mind, I discovered to my relief and delight that it *was* a gun in his pocket. I lifted it from inside his jacket, turned and fired in one elegant and I have to admit well-practised movement.

Yes, I felt sorry for the Hanks. But there again, they were dead already thanks to Max. One of them I'm sure already had wrinkles spreading across his forehead. But it was difficult to tell with a hole through it.

My second shot was so close to the first it could have been an echo. In which case it was the shadow of a bullet that drilled through Second Hank's blazer and stained it red as my lips.

A hand grabbed me from behind, pulling me backwards.

It was Max – after another kiss. His eyes were wide with infatuation and he was breathing heavily while sweating profusely. I shrugged out of his embrace, crouching low – very low in fact – to escape his arms, while simultaneously sweeping the Third Hank's legs from under him with my own.

He crashed face-down to the floor. As he tried to get up again, Max Kliener stepped on his head in his hurry to get at me, lips revoltingly puckered. The noise Hank's head made when it connected with the hard floor was almost as revolting. He didn't get up after that.

'Mr Kliener...' the final Hank called from over by the door. He seemed unsure what to do.

'Out!' Max yelled at him.

Hank didn't move, just stared in disbelief.

'Get out – leave us in peace, can't you? Me and Miss Malone have...' His eyebrows crept so far up his forehead they threatened to become a replacement hairline. '...business.'

I was tempted to ask him to stay. But Hank was out of the door like a rabbit out of an electrified hat.

Unfortunately that left me alone with Max Kliener. The effect of my lipstick-kiss was that I had exchanged death for what is sometimes termed 'a fate worse than death'. Opinions differ, I'm sure. But, whatever the relative merits of death versus Max-kiss, I was pretty keen to avoid both.

'Melody!' he enthused.

'Mr Kliener,' I said warily, backing away.

'Please call me Max.'

'Please call me a taxi.'

He didn't find that as pithy and amusing as many would. I thought it was quite good under the circumstances. But I was unpleasantly aware that backing away from Kliener's clutching fingers was bringing me closer and closer to the Angel.

The bodies of all three Hanks were disintegrating as I tried not to watch. Kliener didn't notice at all and cared even less. His bulging eyes were fixed on me and my own bulges. His henchmen crumbled to dust around us as the Angel drew more and more energy. It would take more than that before she could move far or fast enough to be a real danger. But she'd get there.

Not that the Angel needed to move at all if Kliener kept coming at me. It was a straight choice between being smothered by his (let's say) enthusiasm, or the deadly touch of the creature made of pitted stone. A straight choice maybe, but not an easy one.

'Melody – you're just playing hard to get.'

'Hard as nails,' I agreed.

'All I want is a kiss. Just one more little kiss. I ain't never been kissed like that before.'

Even if I ignored the double-negative, it sounded like I'd overdone the lipstick.

Not that Max cared. 'It was the kiss of an *angel.*'

His lips protruding alarmingly, Kliener closed his eyes into tight scrunches, and leaped at me from point-blank range.

If he thought I was going to stand there meekly and give in to the puckered-lips apocalypse, he was sadly mistaken.

'I'm no angel,' I said, and stepped to one side with a neatness and poise that would have impressed a prima ballerina. Well, Max Kliener should relate to *that.*

At the moment, however, he had other things to relate to. With me out of the way, he overbalanced, tripped, staggered a few steps forwards, and found himself in the arms of and kissing a very different sort of angel.

He seemed to freeze in position. The Angel was very definitely smiling now. Her face was undeniably less weathered, her wings less chipped and fractured.

Max Kliener looked grey, as if all the colour had been sapped from him. His face was lined and cracked like ancient stone. Then he simply crumbled away. A scattering of dust fell to the floor at the stone Angel's feet. Followed by a well-chewed cigar.

Chapter 9
Closing the Case

At the end of every case there are a few loose ends to tidy away. Sometimes more than others. This one was probably about average. I drew the curtain on the Angel rather than let her watch me work: She'd be quite safe out of sight against the back wall of the building, I decided. Oh, she was strong enough to move about a bit, but not beyond the curtain. Now might be a good opportunity to refer back to my comments on hindsight in the sort of way that, at the time, I didn't.

My concern was more human. The last remaining Hank was a problem that would resolve itself, sadly. The current Giddy Semestre and Rock Railton too. Also sadly. Hatchet-faced Hilda the Make-Up Lady was a different prospect, but maybe she'd see an opportunity in the studio's inevitable demise and apply her talents to her own features. It couldn't hurt.

But in the meantime I could do something for the poor unfortunates trapped in their bell jars.

I had a smashing time getting them all out. The first was the most difficult because I had no help. But I dragged a Rock Railton to the coffin-shaped tank, and then got to work on the equipment. I'm pretty good with a screwdriver. I don't mean the drink, though actually, now I come to think of it...

One thing that had puzzled me was how an oaf like Kliener could possibly have created such a device. I soon found my answer – he hadn't. It was just a collection of wires and valves arranged with the haphazard 'try it and see' mentality of a hopeful dullard. The Angel had simply given Kliener what he wanted. The Angel, not the equipment, did all the work. And, arrogant to a degree that eclipsed whatever common sense he once had, Kliener assumed he had created the machinery. Maybe the Angel planted the idea in his rather empty head in the first place.

But whatever the case, it meant I had merely to reconnect the cables the other way round. I suffered a slight crisis of conscience (all such crises are slight in my book), before switching on.

My twinge, let's call it that, was because I didn't actually know which of the Rock Railton copies had been created from which of the original men that the equipment had stored details for.

When the process was finished, and I helped a confused and rather tired-looking young man out of the tank, he might have got someone else's features and body again. Or he might be back to himself. I consoled myself with the knowledge that he would never actually know. Whoever he was now was the person he thought and remembered he had always been.

I don't know what he made of the process of helping me carry another unconscious body over to the tank. But as it was a Giddy Semestre copy, he probably quite enjoyed it.

It wasn't too long before the bell jars were empty and an assortment of confused young men and women listened to me explain about experimental movie effects, thank them for their help, and talk in brief about where they could find out more about training for the stunt industry. I doubt any of them were impressed. None of them seemed keen to follow up on my suggestion that Max Kliener would be happy to explain *everything*.

I watched them leave. They were young and mostly good looking, but there wasn't a Rock Railton or a Giddy Semestre among them. They were all of a similar height and roughly the same build as the stars they had been intended to replace, but they just didn't have... something. Maybe it's star quality. Maybe it's charisma. Maybe it's just confidence.

But they were all alive and well. They'd not been kissed by an angel, so they'd live full and happy lives. Or as full and happy as fate decreed. They were all unique, all – in their own special way and to someone – a *star*.

As soon as I was alone, I dismantled the equipment

and got to work again with my screwdriver. Soon it was just a pile of metal, cables, wires and tubes. I'd call by the prop store on my way out and have them just take it away.

That left only the Angel to deal with. How do you deal with a statue, that had to be the real problem. Only, of course, it wasn't.

The real problem, as I discovered when I pulled back the curtain, was finding it again. Where the Angel had been standing, there was an empty space. In front of the empty space was a faint dusting of Max Kliener. Behind it was a large hole in the wall where someone had taken out one of the prefabricated panels from the outside.

I knew this because the actual panel had been carefully – and obviously quietly – leaned up against the wall beside the resulting hole. Several sets of footmarks in the dust and dirt led away from the building. It must have happened while I was preoccupied with ushering out the confused and rather noisy Starlight Stars and Starlets. In the distance I could see a trail of dust kicked up by a departing truck. A truck that was undoubtedly taking the Angel away to...

Well, that was the question, wasn't it?

One case might be over, but another had just opened. New York was growling outside, but I was ready for it. My stocking seams were straight, my lipstick was combat-ready, and I was packing cleavage that could fell an ox at twenty feet.

What had happened to the Angel was a mystery.

But I am Melody Malone, with ice in my heart and a kiss on my lips. In the city that never sleeps and should never blink, mysteries are my business.

*The Lizard Woman, the Troll
and the Parlour Maid in*

Devil in the Smoke

*An Adventure for the Great Detective
Recounted by Mr Justin Richards*

The First Chapter

*In which a strange and grisly death
is revealed...*

Madame Vastra, the fabled Lizard Woman of
Paternoster Row, knew death in many shapes and
forms. But perhaps one of the most bizarre of these
was death by snow.

It was a cold day in December, just as the
nineteenth century was greying with old age. The
snow was falling less heavily than on previous
days, but the air was still alive with a coruscation of
dancing flakes.

Tired of sweeping snow from the workhouse
yard, Harry and Jim (surnames unknown even to
themselves) decided instead to make a snowman.
Knowing Mr Ransit to be availing himself of the
benefits of a hot fire in the workhouse offices, they
left the yard to fend for itself for a few hours.

In a secluded corner of Ranskill Gardens,
unobserved by passers-by, they set about their task.
They worked hard, struggling to keep warm in the

inclement conditions. They started with a small ball of packed snow, rolling it along the ground. It gathered more and more snow as it went, getting larger and larger. Before long, the two young lads had rolled a snowball ample enough to form the body of their creation.

A short while later, and a smaller snowball formed the head. Between them, they lifted it and placed it on top of the body. The snowman was now taller than they were, so the task of balancing frosty head on snowy shoulders was not straightforward. Pieces of coal from Jim's pocket made eyes, and pebbles from the edge of a nearby flowerbed served as buttons down the snowman's front, pressed into the cold, yielding body.

A broken carrot, saved for the purpose with admirable forethought by young Harry, was positioned as the snowman's nose. Beneath it, he described a smiling mouth with his finger.

'It's a shame we don't have a hat for him,' Jim opined.

'Give him your cap,' Harry suggested.

'Give him yours,' Jim retorted.

'Nah,' Harry decided. 'Don't reckon Mr Snowman will feel the cold.'

They both laughed at this, and before long an impromptu snowball fight had started between the two.

Finally, cold, soaked and exhausted, the two boys sat down in front of the snowman and admired their handiwork. As they sat there, the afternoon drawing into early evening, there was a crackle as if of gunfire followed by a percussion of lights and sparks in the sky above.

'Fireworks!' Harry exclaimed.

'Must be left over from November the fifth,' Jim observed. 'We had that weeks ago.'

'Or Christmas has come early.'

They watched the display for several minutes. At some point – he could not say exactly when – Harry observed that a dark figure wearing a top hat had appeared in the corner of the gardens behind their snowman. He too seemed to be watching the display. As the last few fireworks exploded in the evening sky, the man pushed something Harry could not clearly see into his coat pocket, turned, and stepped back into the shadows by the back wall of the gardens.

'Who was that?' Harry asked.

But Jim had seen no one. 'Probably come to admire our snowman. Here,' he added as a final explosive crack echoed round the enclosed space, 'we'd better be getting back. Still got that yard to sweep.'

At least now the snow had stopped falling they could sweep the yard without it merely filling up again, Harry thought. But before they left, the two boys paused to admire their snowman one last time.

It was taller than either of them, and wider than both of them together. They were about to turn, reluctantly, and leave, when a portion of snow fell away from the front of the frosty sculpture. Two of the pebble-buttons fell with it. Jim retrieved them and pressed them back into the snowman's chest.

'Wonder if he'll still be here tomorrow,' Harry said.

But Jim did not reply. The boy was staring at his index finger – the one with which he had pressed the pebbles into the snow.

The end of his finger was a livid red. Even in the fading light of the evening, Harry could see what it was.

'Blood! You cut yourself, Jim?'

Jim shook his head. He looked at his finger, then to the snowman. His gasp of horrified astonishment drew Harry's attention back to the white figure.

Where Jim had pressed one of the pebbles into the chest, the snow was stained red. A patch of scarlet was spreading slowly through the icy crystals.

'The snowman!' Harry gasped. 'It's – it's *bleeding*!'

Not only bleeding, the snowman was *moving*. The body seemed to shimmer. Frosty particles broke free and fell to the ground. Drops of red broke free of the wound, undulating down the snowman in thin streams of viscous carmine.

Tentatively, fearfully, Jim reached out to touch the snowman. As soon as his fingers met the frozen surface, the snowman seemed to *explode*. Snow collapsed from round the core of the body, falling away to reveal what was inside.

The boys stood frozen by fear as well as the cold. They had made this snowman – had rolled the snow to make the body and then the head. How could what they now witnessed be possible?

Because, inside the snowman, packed deep into its frozen heart, was the body of a woman. Her features were deathly pale, her coat stained with blood. Her gloved hands were clenched together in front of her, reaching out as if pleading for help or praying for salvation.

But it was too late and there was no help to be given or salvation to be had. Because as Harry and Jim watched, the woman inside the snowman collapsed lifeless to the frozen ground before them.

They both ran. Without thought or strategy they took to their heels to put as much distance between themselves and this grotesque impossibility as possible, their caps flying from their heads, such was their haste. But in the fading light, fearing for their very lives, somehow they became separated from each other.

Jim found himself in an unfamiliar street, behind Ranskill Gardens. Running fast, head down, he collided with someone before he even knew they were there. He stumbled and fell to the snowy ground.

'Here, let me help you up.' A dark figure reached down to him. Jim saw only a silhouette – dark coat and top hat. Then a gloved hand closed on his own and hauled him to his feet.

'Now,' the figure said, 'where are you going in such a hurry, young man?'

Harry had run in a different direction. But he too

collided with a dark figure. He too fell to the ground. His cap went flying, but Harry made no move to recover it.

The figure Harry had met was shorter, broader, wearing a heavy black cloak with the hood pulled up to obscure its features. Powerful hands clamped down on Harry's shoulders and lifted him bodily to his feet. Harry was surprised to observe that, despite his evident strength, the figure was barely as tall as he was.

An unsettling grunt of satisfaction emerged from the hood of the cloak.

'You are not a female,' a gravelly voice said.

'No – no, sir,' Harry admitted.

'Where is the female?' the cloaked figure demanded.

In Harry's mind at that moment there were thoughts of only one female. 'She's dead,' he stammered. 'We made a snowman, and she fell out – dead.' He doubled over, feeling suddenly sick. 'Oh my cripes,' he gasped. 'I ain't never seen anything so…'

As he spoke, he looked up at the figure standing in front of him. It moved slightly so that the light from the nearest gas lamp shone inside the hood of the cloak and illuminated the visage concealed within.

It was the hideous misshapen face of a troll.

The Second Chapter

*In which Harry meets a troll and feasts
on soup and bread...*

The creature – for it was surely a creature rather than
a man – stared at Harry through small, deep-set dark
eyes. A bloodless tongue licked equally bloodless
lips. The face was entirely devoid of hair, wider than
it was high, and seemed to emerge directly from the
shoulders without the beneficial support of a neck.

Harry took a step backwards, ready to turn and
run from the nightmare apparition before him.
But the 'troll' grabbed him by the shoulders again,
holding him fast in an iron grip.

'Explain,' the troll hissed.

'Explain what? I was just...' Harry pointed back
the way he'd come. 'Let me go, please, sir. I won't
breathe a word about what I seen. Not about you nor
the dead body.'

'Explain the dead body,' the troll said, shaking
Harry so violently that his teeth rattled.

'It's a body,' he said when he could finally draw

breath. 'And it's dead. A woman, in a coat, bleeding.'

'What colour fur?' the troll demanded.

'It's not fur, it's probably wool.'

The creature's eyes narrowed even further. 'Not the coat,' it rasped. 'On its head – what colour was the fur on the female's head?'

Harry frowned, struggling to understand. 'You mean her hair?'

'Hair, fur, protective cranial grafting – whatever term you use on this primitive planet. What colour was it?'

'Sort of... brownish.'

'Brownish.'

'And quite long. I think.' Despite the tight grip that the troll maintained on his shoulders, Harry managed to get one hand up high enough to show how long the dead woman's hair had been. 'About this long.'

The grip on his shoulders loosened and Harry felt himself sag. Then he stumbled forwards under a near-crippling slap on his back.

'Good lad,' the troll said. 'Your observational skills are adequate. You would make a good forward sniper.'

'Oh, um, thank you, sir.' Harry swallowed. 'Can I go now?'

'No.'

'Why not?'

'You must deliver your report in person. The probability is that it has a significant bearing on the matter in hand. Come with me.'

Harry hesitated. The troll had raised his own hand as he spoke – and Harry saw that it was a hand that boasted only three fingers. Or possibly two fingers and a thumb.

'Where are we going, sir?'

The troll regarded him in the manner which a nanny might reserve for an especially slow-witted infant. 'To Paternoster Row,' he said, as if that should be obvious. 'To see the Great Detective.'

And with that, the troll caught hold of the back of Harry's coat and lifted him with one hand to carry him down the street towards a waiting carriage.

Harry's plan, such as he had one, was to climb into the carriage then immediately out again on the other side, and so escape the inhuman clutches of the troll. It was a trick he had worked before with some effect. But on this occasion, lamentably, it was destined to fail.

The troll opened the carriage door with his free hand and hurled Harry inside. The boy landed upside down on the seat, his feet grazing the upholstered ceiling of what was indeed a rather plush conveyance.

Harry's plan was thwarted the moment he managed to grasp the handle of the door – it was locked. The carriage started moving at speed, rattling over the cobbles, and Harry found himself being flung unceremoniously around the carriage interior.

As the carriage lurched around another steep

corner, he contrived to fall towards the door through which he had entered. But this egress too was secured. For the duration, Harry was trapped inside, tumbling back and forth as the troll drove like a veritable demon through the London streets.

After several minutes, Harry could do nothing but resign himself to the journey and give thanks that the interior of the carriage was so heavily padded.

Harry had never been on a ship, or even the smallest river boat. But by the time the carriage drew to a halt, he felt certain he knew what sea sickness must feel like. It was not a positive experience by any measure.

He did not have long to recover, however, between the termination of the vehicle's motion and the door opening. A pair of inhuman hands reached in and hauled him out, upside down. He was then placed – in an upright orientation, mercifully – on the pavement.

The troll grunted something that ended with: '... after you.'

'That's kind,' Harry managed to say.

The troll stared at him, lip curling slightly. 'I said: "If you run I shall come after you."' The hairless ogre gave Harry a shove in the direction of the front door of the nearest house.

It was a tall townhouse, with steps up to the main entrance. Harry staggered up, and the troll reached past him to pull the bell. It jangled distantly within the domicile.

To Harry's surprise, the door was opened not by

another creature drawn from the realms of nightmare and fantasy, but by a very ordinary-looking maid servant. Ordinary, but even to Harry's juvenile sensibilities decidedly pretty, with dark hair. The only thing about her that might have derived from a fantastical creature of myth or folklore was her imp-ish smile.

Her manner and tone, however, was decidedly earthly. 'Cor strewth, Strax,' she intoned, 'how many times do I have to tell you the difference between a lady and a fellah?'

'I know the difference full well, boy,' the troll told her. Without waiting for further comment, he shoved Harry though the door into a well-apportioned if slightly narrow hallway.

The straitened nature of the vestibule was of no concern to either the maid or Harry, but he saw that Strax, as the maid had addressed the troll, took some trouble negotiating the doorway and subsequent side table, ornaments, and other bespoke furnishings.

Ignoring the crash of breaking china, the maid ushered Harry into a large drawing room. He hurried over to the fire to warm himself while the maid and the troll argued in the doorway.

'He is a witness. I have brought him to give his report,' Strax said.

'His report? Into what – mistaken identity and child abduction?'

'No, into… *murder.*'

'Murder – whose murder?' The maid put her hands on her hips and stared at Strax through eyes even narrower than the troll himself had deployed. 'Who did you kill?'

'No one,' Strax insisted. 'Well, no one *recently*.'

'It weren't him,' Harry called out. As much as correcting a possible injustice, he felt he should remind them of his presence. 'It were a lady. Killed inside my snowman – well,' he admitted, 'mine and Jim's snowman. We made it,' he said proudly. Then his face crumpled as he remembered. 'And this dead body fell out of it. All covered in blood and everything.'

And with that, the full enormity of his situation finally came home to Harry, and he sank to the heavy pile carpet in a flood of tears.

The maid introduced herself as Jenny Flint, and she brought Harry a bowl of hot soup with thick slices of warm, fresh bread. To eat it he sat at a table that was bigger than the area he had to live in at the workhouse. The wood was so highly polished he could see his face reflected in it. Grimy and tear-streaked, he realised that he looked as out of place in this establishment as did the troll-like Strax.

'So who are you?' Harry demanded as Jenny sat and watched him eat.

The words were rather indistinct, spoken as they were though a mouthful of bread.

Jenny dabbed at the soup and breadcrumbs now strewn across the table with the napkin which Harry had spurned.

'I told you, I'm Jenny. And don't mind Strax – his

bark's worse than his bite.'

'He's a dog?'

'No, course not. And actually…' Jenny frowned. 'Actually his bite is probably worse than his bark. Forget I said that. We both work for…' She paused to bring home the full effect of her next words. 'The Great Detective.'

Harry nodded. 'That's nice.'

'You never heard of the Great Detective?' Jenny asked.

'Sherlock Holmes, isn't he? But everyone knows that's just a story.'

Jenny sniffed and did some more napkin-mopping. 'Not *that* great detective. A *real* one. Madame Vastra.'

Harry shook his head. He'd never heard of her.

'Just so long as she ain't another troll or ogre or anything.'

Jenny smiled. 'She's nothing like Strax, if that's what you mean.'

As she spoke, there came the sound of the front door slamming shut.

'That'll be her now,' Jenny said. 'I'd better go and explain that the guest we have staying ain't the guest she was expecting.'

Harry finished his soup alone. He could hear voices in the hallway outside – Jenny and another woman. He could not make out the words, but the other woman sounded friendly and warm. Harry finished the last of the bread, wiped his mouth carefully on the tablecloth, and got up from the table.

Jenny was standing in the hallway. The other woman – who could only be the aforementioned Madame Vastra – had her back to Harry. She was wearing a cape with a hood, not unlike Strax. But Madame Vastra's attire evidently covered a taller, more elegant and feminine figure.

Then Madame Vastra turned, and Harry saw her face.

It was green, and scaled in the manner of a cold-blooded reptile. Her eyes were slanted cat-like, and a long, forked tongue hung from her thin lips.

It was the face of the fabled Lizard Woman.

The Third Chapter

In which a killing is narrowly averted
and swords are crossed...

The spectacle of this second monstrous apparition, to say nothing of his earlier cognition of mortality, was too much for young Harry. With a cry of surprise laced liberally with fear, he turned and ran down the hall – away from the lizard woman and the maid.

Harry's flight took him past the main staircase and into the rearmost area of the house that would normally have been the domain of the servants. While he lacked foreknowledge of the domestic topography, by some instinct Harry found himself in the scullery from whence an outer door opened into the backyard.

But it was not all to be plain sailing, for there was another individual already at work in the scullery. Elbow-deep in an enamelled sink, the squat figure of Strax was to be found engaged in the latter stages of washing dishes. A pile of broken crockery stacked precariously on the drainer bore witness to his particular unsuitability for the task.

Harry spared no time to ponder on the allocation of household chores and hurried past Strax and out through the door. Behind him he could hear Jenny the maid shouting for Strax to 'Stop that boy!' Once in the yard he spared no time negotiating the falling snow in order to find a convenient exit. This achieved, he set off along a narrow passageway that led back to the street.

Despite having not the slightest idea of where in London he might be, Harry kept running. He could hear the heavy, measured tread of Strax behind him. But the sound, like Harry's form, was muffled and obscured by the thickening snow that had filled the air and obscured the vision as evening drew in. So it was that Harry was able to stay ahead and out of sight of his pursuers.

There was but one thought in the young lad's mind, which was to find his way back to the workhouse. He might find himself castigated for failing to complete the sweeping of the yard, but this was likely to be preferable to remaining in the company of the Lizard Woman, the Troll and the Parlour Maid.

That said, he was in no small part grateful for the soup. This still exerted a warming sensation, which to some degree compensated for Harry's lack of coat, this garment being left over the back of a chair in the drawing room at Paternoster Row.

It was not therefore surprising that, notwithstanding Jenny's ministrations, he was shivering with cold and slick with a coating of snow by the time he reached a street that he recognised. Despite the thickening white-out, Harry realised that he was not far from the workhouse. With a measure of trepidation as well as relief, he upped his pace, and before long saw the unforgiving walls of the corrective establishment rising above him.

However, at that self-same moment, he heard the clatter of a carriage on the cobbles. Fearing the worst, Harry withdrew himself into a shadowed alcove in the wall. These worst fears were confirmed when he saw that the coachman driving the carriage was a squat, cloaked figure blessed with but three fingers on the hand in which he held the reins. From out of the carriage window, Jenny's face peered through the falling curtain of white flakes.

Of course, Harry realised, Strax would know that there was a workhouse not two streets from where he had encountered the boy. It would not take the mind of a genius to deduce this must be where Harry was from and therefore might well return. Even if the mind of Strax was not up to this menial mental task, Jenny or the enigmatic Madame Vastra had evidently made the connection.

Another connection was also made – this one between Jenny's eyes and the sight of Harry attempting to remain unseen in the shadow of the workhouse wall.

'There he is,' she said to Madame Vastra, who sat cloaked and veiled beside her within the conveyance.

Vastra raised her voice to call up to Strax. 'Keep

going to the end of the street. We cannot alarm the boy.'

'I can,' Strax called back. 'Would you like me to start now?'

'No,' the lizard lady replied with enviable calm. 'I would rather he was not scared for his life. We must win his trust.'

'I thought hot soup would do that,' Jenny opined.

'Evidently something more is needed.'

The carriage drew to a halt. Satisfied that its form would be obscured by the omnipresent snow, Madame Vastra disembarked and led the way back to where they had seen Harry pressed back against the wall.

Of the boy, there was no sign. But two other figures – larger figures – were in evidence hurrying from the scene. Although they were vague figures glimpsed but briefly, several things were at once apparent to Jenny and Madame Vastra.

The first was that the men were in some haste, and the second that they were themselves in pursuit of another individual. Neither the lizard nor the maid were in any doubt as to who that individual might be.

'What's he got himself into?' Jenny wondered.

'I think perhaps we should find out,' her mistress decided. 'Tell Strax to secure the carriage, and then follow me. I shall help the boy.'

'You think he's in danger?' Jenny asked.

But Vastra was already disappearing into the snow, so with a sigh Jenny turned and ran back to the waiting carriage. She quickly explained to Strax what they had witnessed.

'I shall break out the heavy weapons,' Strax informed her.

'We didn't bring any heavy weapons,' Jenny pointed out.

'I may have some things that could be of use,' Strax replied. One of them turned out to be nosebags for the horses. Another was long, metallic, and very sharp.

The road that Jenny had seen Vastra take in pursuit of the two men led down towards the docks. This was not an area that Jenny would ordinarily elect to explore. Although she was certainly well able to take care of herself, there was some value, she had to admit, in Strax's company.

Young Harry, meanwhile, would have been appreciative of any company. He had run as soon as the two men loomed out of the swirling snow. While he did not know what they intended, he was well able to discern on whom they intended to inflict it. They approached him wearing unpleasant grins, and one of them hefted a brutal-looking wooden cudgel.

Harry's plan, formulated at the speed of fright, was to lose himself in the docks. If he was lucky, the men wished merely to give him a beating and relieve him of whatever coinage he might happen to have about his person. In that case, if he could keep ahead of them, then they were likely to search for easier pickings elsewhere.

However, it seemed from the tenacity of their pursuit that they might have more sinister intentions towards the person of Harry in particular. Worn down by the cold and his previous exertions, he was unable to escape. A calloused hand descended on Harry's collar and snapped him violently backwards.

Both men soon had hold of Harry and seemed intent on beating him to within an inch of his young life. He found himself shoved up against a brick wall with such vigour that the breath was forced from his lungs and he doubled up, winded.

'What did you see?' one of the men demanded. He held the cudgel under Harry's chin, pushing him up onto his tiptoes. His misty breath mingled with the gathering fog. 'Tell us everything you saw.'

'I didn't see nothing,' Harry exclaimed, though he had no idea to what the men were specifically referring.

'So you did see something,' the second man proclaimed, taking Harry's speed of denial as an indication of a corresponding lack of veracity.

'What – when? I dunno what you're on about,' Harry protested.

'The boss won't be very happy with you,' the first man said. He pulled back the cudgel, ready to strike.

'What boss?' Harry blurted. But he was not to get an answer.

Instead there was the sound of something slicing rapidly through the heavy air. Harry braced himself for the blow. It never came. For the sound was a sword which struck the cudgel from the ruffian's grasp and sent it clattering away across the cobbles.

Harry's eyes opened wide in surprise.

The men turned and their own eyes also widened, but in their cases due to fear.

Madame Vastra held her sword in a fighting stance, ready to strike again. The hood of her cloak hung forward, occluding her features.

'There's just the one of them,' the second ruffian said. 'We can match her.'

'Can't you count?' another voice said.

To Harry's delight, Jenny stepped into the light, standing beside Vastra. She was poised on the balls of her feet, her hands clenched into fists and positioned ready to attack.

'Always come prepared for battle,' a third, rather guttural, voice added. 'Even if you do not have time to pack heavy weaponry, experience has shown that small arms and primitive blades can be offensive.' Strax stood with his arms folded between Vastra and Jenny.

'You'd better go,' Vastra said. 'Before he gets even more offensive.' So saying, she threw back her head so that the hood was dislodged and fell back upon her shoulders.

The sight of the lizard woman's visage together with Strax's ogre-esque features proved too much for the men's depleted courage. They backed slowly away, one of them reaching to cuff Harry about the head. But the boy managed to duck beneath the blow and run to join Vastra and the others.

'You breathe a word to anyone about what you saw and you're dead meat,' the thug grunted, pointing at Harry. 'You wait till the boss finds you.'

Vastra stepped forward. 'You harm one hair on the head of this mammal pup,' she said, 'and your own head will immediately be forfeit in return.' She raised the sword by way of emphasis.

The sound of the men's running footsteps was interrupted only by Strax's grunt of satisfaction.

'You are blessed with luck, small one,' he told Harry. 'Rejoice and give thanks – someone wants you dead.'

The Fourth Chapter

*In which ale is imbibed and Harry
is reunited with a friend…*

With young Harry held firmly in Strax's grasp, the group made their way out of the docks area and paused to collect their thoughts at a hostelry known to Madame Vastra. The Crofter's Arms had a quiet back room where Vastra knew she and her friends would attract less attention than in the public bar.

Thus, away from the bibulous gaze of the masses, Vastra was able to enjoy a dry sherry while Jenny outraged convention by demanding a cup of tea, and Strax drained a pint of the landlord's finest Old Rotter in a single gulp. Harry made do with warm milk.

Once they were all settled, Madame Vastra assured Harry that she and the others were concerned only with his safety. 'I may look strange and Strax here would frighten even the most lethargic cow, but we are your friends.'

Harry nodded and said nothing.

Jenny put her hand over his. 'She's all right, is Madame Vastra. And Strax too...' She spared him a sideways glance. 'In his own way.'

'The cub will not be safe at the working house,' Strax said. 'The walls are strong but the construction is not ideal for defensive engagements.'

'I agree,' Madame Vastra said, 'and so I think Harry must stay with us at Paternoster Row until this matter is dealt with.'

'You all right with that, Harry?' Jenny asked.

'Mr Ransit will do his noggin,' Harry muttered. He hardly dared imagine what horrors must already be awaiting him back at the workhouse. He longed to see Jim again... Which made him suddenly think: 'Ere – you reckon it's cos of the snowman we made that those men wanted to do away with me?'

'It does seem likely,' Madame Vastra agreed. 'The dead woman was, we believe, Felicity Gregson. She had arranged to meet me at Ranskill Gardens this evening. Unable to keep the appointment, owing to an unfortunate double booking at the Greek Embassy, I sent Strax to fetch her.'

'I was too late,' Strax said sullenly, leaping to his feet and standing smartly to attention. 'I failed in my task. I will submit myself for court martial and summary execution forthwith. I suggest coronic acid immersion followed by a laser-pulse blast to the probic vent.'

Vastra, who was used to these outbursts of aggressive contrition, raised her hand. 'That will not be necessary, Strax.'

Strax seemed perhaps disappointed, and slumped back down in his chair.

'But what about Jim?' Harry blurted out.

'Who?' Jenny asked.

'My friend Jim. We built the snowman together. We both saw the dead woman. If they're after me – what about Jim?'

Madame Vastra sipped her sherry and considered. 'The ruffians who accosted you now know that we are involved and that you will have told us what you saw. Assuming that is why they attacked you, then they must know that the information they sought to suppress is now more widely held.'

'They may be prepared to inflict collateral damage,' Strax said. 'Perhaps,' he added with some relish, 'we are *all* at risk.'

'No, no – hang about. They mentioned a boss,' Jenny pointed out.

'They were obviously working for someone, my dear,' Vastra agreed.

'But what if that someone doesn't know about us yet. What if they think Harry's dead, like they ordered.'

'What if they do?' Strax seemed not at all interested in the boy's fate. 'Casualties must be expected.'

Vastra was shaking her green, scaly head. 'No, Jenny is right. If the mysterious boss believes Harry has been silenced, then it seems likely he would make similar arrangements for this other witness.'

'But witness to what?' Jenny wondered.

'Never mind all that,' Harry told them. 'If Jim's in

trouble, we got to help him, and now.'

Vastra drained the last of her sherry and set the glass down sharply on the table. 'I agree. Will this Jim have returned to the workhouse, as you did?'

Harry nodded. 'I reckon so.'

'Then there is no time to lose. Jenny, settle the tab for the drinks. Strax, make all haste to the workhouse and keep watch. And you, Harry – tell me everything you can remember about poor Miss Felicity Gregson and how she met her fate. Spare no detail. The slightest clue could be of immense help.'

As they made their hurried way back to the workhouse, Harry recounted his story once again. It was only when Madame Vastra asked him if he was sure that there were no other witnesses to the bizarre spectacle of the corpse within the snowman, that he recalled the shadowy figure he had seen behind the snowman, watching them.

Vastra listened to his description, then told him to relate what had happened next. So Harry told her about how he and Jim had both run, but in different directions, and how he had cannoned into Strax.

By now, Jenny had caught up with them and they were approaching the familiar but stark form of the workhouse. Harry did not relish the prospect of explaining his absence to Mr Ransit, and was therefore mightily relieved when Madame Vastra suggested that he wait in the nearby carriage.

'Strax and I will check the immediate area,' she said. 'Jenny – you will see this Mr Ransit.'

'Right-oh, Ma'am,' Jenny agreed. 'And what do I tell him?'

'That Harry is now in our charge. Make sure he releases him to you as guardian, at least until these unpleasant matters are concluded. If the boy Jim is there, then we will need him released into our care too. I imagine an exchange of currency may be necessary. After that, it will be time to find out what really happened in Ranskill Gardens this evening, and perhaps go on the offensive.'

Strax slammed his fist into the open palm of his other hand. 'At last,' he pronounced. 'We strike for the greater glory of the Sontaran Empire. Sontar-Ha!' His brow furrowed slightly as he saw the others' expressions. 'That is, for the greater glory of Paternoster Row, of course. Pater-Nos-Ta!'

Madame Vastra raised what might have been an eyebrow.

Sitting alone in the well-appointed carriage, Harry began to feel at ease for the first time since he and Jim had completed their snowman and seen the fireworks. He settled back into the plush upholstery and closed his eyes. So it was that he assumed he must have slipped into slumber and be dreaming when someone hissed close to his ear:

'Psssst!'

He ignored this susurration, turning slightly away.

'Oi – Harry!' The words were punctuated by a frantic rapping on the carriage door.

To Harry's surprise, when he opened his eyes he saw a face he recognised staring in through the adjacent window.

'Jim!' he exclaimed in delight. 'Are you all right? Where have you been? You'll never guess what happened to me.'

Harry tore open the carriage door so that his friend could climb in and join him.

'I had to warn you,' Jim said, looking around warily.

'Warn me? Too late for that,' Harry responded. 'These two geezers already tried to do for me tonight.'

'Never mind them,' Jim said. 'They're not the real villains of the piece.'

'Then who is?' Perhaps Jim was about to reveal the name of the villains' mysterious employer.

'It's the lizard woman and her lot,' Jim said.

'Never!'

Harry was about to explain how Vastra had helped him. But Jim went on: 'Tis and all. She plans to kill you and cook you in a stew, I heard her. She's planning it with the potato-headed man right now.'

This seemed the height of improbability to Harry, and he wasted no time in telling his friend exactly that.

'You don't believe me? Then just you come and listen then. I'll show you the way. Come with me, and you'll find out just how much danger you're really in, right enough. Come on.'

So saying, Jim opened the door and leaped down

from the carriage.

Reluctantly, Harry followed. His friend led the way along the outer wall of the workhouse and into a small square on the other side. The square was bordered on three sides by terraced houses, and on the fourth by the workhouse wall. The snow had eased once more, and fog swirled round the enclosed space. Tendrils teased out by the breeze seemed like long, slender fingers clawing at Harry as he followed Jim to a secluded and shadowy corner.

'So where's Vastra and the others?' Harry demanded. It seemed that there was no one here.

But that was just an illusion. A dark figure detached itself from the shadows and stepped towards Harry. The man seemed dark and vague, as if he had somehow coalesced out of the fog itself.

'I told you that you'd find out how much trouble you're in, Harry,' Jim said. For the first time, Harry noticed how much the boy's voice was trembling. How pale and frightened he looked. 'I'm sorry, but I had to do it.'

'Had to do what?' Harry asked. But deep within his sinking heart he had already deduced the answer.

'Had to bring you to me,' the shadow man pronounced. His voice was deep and cultured. As he approached, Harry realised that this was the man from Ranskill Gardens – the man who had appeared at the same time as the fireworks display. Again the man tapped the brim of his top hat, but this time in greeting rather than valediction.

'But don't blame poor Jim,' the man went on. 'He

brought you to me for a very good reason.'

Before Harry could move, the man's hands whipped out and grabbed him securely by the shoulders. Harry cried out in pain and fear. Fog seemed to seep from open ends of the man's cuffs, curling round his wrists and Harry's shoulders.

'Greater pragmatism has no man than this,' the figure said. 'That he betray his friends to save his own life.'

'What are you going to do with me?' Harry asked, stammering through the pain and the anger.

But the man's only response was his laughter, echoing through the foggy night.

The Fifth Chapter

*In which a mystery
is solved…*

With the disappearance of Harry, there was only one other lead for the Great Detective to follow. Jenny was adamant that the boy would not have run away again.

'He trusted us. He knew he was in danger. Someone's taken him.'

'There is no sign of a siege,' Strax pointed out. 'The carriage is undamaged. No evidence of the deployment of weaponry.'

'The threat may have been enough,' Vastra said. 'Or his abductors may have employed more subtle means.'

Strax grunted. 'Explain "subtle".'

'Don't think you'd understand,' Jenny told him, not unkindly.

Vastra meanwhile had settled herself into the carriage. 'Let us examine,' she said, 'the scene of the original crime.'

*

The body had been discovered and removed from Ranskill Gardens. A lone police constable kept watch, presumably on the understanding that a stable door locked after the equine occupant has vacated the premises is at least more secure than one that is never locked at all.

Jenny engaged the constable in conversation while Madame Vastra examined the scene of the crime. Or, at least, the location where the body of Miss Felicity Gregson had ended up. Strax prowled the immediate neighbourhood, keeping an eye out for anything out of the ordinary and attempting – largely without success – to remain inconspicuous.

Making sure that she was not overlooked, Madame Vastra lifted the dark veil that concealed her reptilian features and examined the churned-up snow. There were splashes of red upon the white, several pebbles, and an incongruous carrot. She moved nothing, letting her fingers – or whatever for a lizard woman passed as fingers – brush gently against the blood. Her keen sense of smell told her at once that it was indeed human...

'Who found her?' Jenny asked the constable. She had already explained that the deceased was an acquaintance who had failed to keep an appointment with her mistress.

'One of the residents. A pathologist himself as luck would have it, Miss. He was able to discern quite quickly that the lady was dead.'

'And how did she die?'

The policeman shifted uncomfortably, stamping

his feet in the snow and blowing on his cold hands. 'I'm not sure that I should divulge that sort of detail.'

'Oh, constable,' Jenny soothed, 'you can tell *me*.'

The constable glanced round, then lowered his voice. 'Well, so long as it goes no further. She was shot, in the back. Her killer must have been quite close, as the bullet went right through.'

'Hence the blood on the front of her coat,' Jenny said thoughtfully, recalling Harry's description of events.

The policeman frowned. 'How could you—'

But Jenny interrupted him before he could complete the thought. 'Were there no witnesses? Did no one hear the shot?'

'Fireworks display, down by the river. Perhaps you saw it, Miss? Made a right old racket, I can tell you. The inspector's theory is that this distracted any attention the sound of a shot might have garnered.'

'And no one saw anything?' Jenny was keen to know if the police were aware of the two boys who had indeed discovered the body before the local pathologist.

The policeman shook his head. 'Was one odd thing, though.'

'Oh yes?'

Behind Jenny, Madame Vastra straightened up from her inspection of the snowy locale and listened keenly.

'Lady in the house that backs onto the corner there.' He paused to indicate the domicile in question. 'She says she saw a man – a gentleman in fact – watching a couple of kids make a snowman.'

'It does look as if there was a snowman here,' Jenny agreed.

'The body was found in the remains of it,' the constable said. 'But that's not the odd thing.'

'Then what is?'

'Well, she swears she recognised the man, though he was muffled up against the cold and wearing a top hat. She says she is sure that it was Able Hecklington, the noted industrialist.' The policeman gave a short laugh. 'Though Lord knows why he'd be hanging about here watching kids make a snowman.'

Back at Paternoster Row, fortified by the remains of the hot soup that had previously restored young Harry, Madame Vastra, Jenny and Strax discussed what they had learned.

'It is obvious what happened,' Vastra said.

This was indeed news to both Strax and Jenny, who were still befuddled by the enigmatic appearance of a dead body within the snowman.

'And,' Vastra went on, 'we now know the identity of the murderer.'

Again, Jenny and Strax exchanged confused looks.

'But how can a dead body just appear inside a snowman?' Jenny asked. 'Harry and his friend Jim made it – they'd have noticed if they were building a snowman round a corpse.'

'Osmic projection,' Strax said knowingly. 'Set the frequency modulator accurately enough and the body appears inside the snow.'

'Not osmic projection,' Vastra told him.

'Then the woman was executed in a pit beneath the snowman. Careful use of a laser cutter would allow the ground to be removed and the cadaver inserted upright into the snowman.'

'Not a laser cutter,' Vastra said with the merest hint of waning patience.

'In that case,' Strax said, undeterred by his audience's lack of enthusiasm, 'the answer is obvious.' He nodded to emphasize how clever he had been to deduce the solution to this singular puzzle. 'Transmutation of matter.'

Jenny frowned. 'You what?'

'Cellular mutation,' Strax told her. 'The crystalline lattice of the snowman's interior was transposed to a DNA-based organic matrix. The woman was created inside the snowman. She was,' he explained, '*made of snow*.'

'No,' Vastra said. 'She was not.'

'However it was done,' Strax said, 'we should find every snowman in London – and *obliterate* them. Just to be on the safe side.'

'So how was it done? What did happen?' Jenny asked.

Madame Vastra leaned back in her chair and clasped her hands in front of her on the table, for all the world like Sherlock Holmes. Only female. And green.

'Miss Gregson was shot in the back.'

'We know that from the police constable at

Ranskill Gardens,' Jenny agreed.

'She was on her way to see me, when she realised she was in danger,' Madame Vastra continued. She stared into the distance, as if seeing the events she described actually unfold...

Felicity Gregson was being followed. She caught a glimpse of her pursuer in the window of a haberdasher's on Ghent Street, and ducked into an alley. The snow was getting heavy again, stinging her eyes as she stared out into the street. There was no sign of the man in the top hat, but she knew he was there. She knew he was watching.

Despite the snow, a thin hint of fog curled like smoke round Felicity's feet. She watched it for a moment, mouth open in surprise and alarm. Then she ran.

At the end of the alley, she turned into another street. Her destination was not far now, and she prayed the person (if person she be) that she was meeting would be there waiting. If anyone could help her...

A glance over her shoulder told her that the man in the top hat was still following. He seemed to solidify behind her out of the very air. Was it her imagination, or did the last few flakes of the ebbing snow fall *through* him as it danced and twisted down to the ground?

She doubled back on her route, took sudden side streets, did her best to get away from the man. By the time she reached Ranskill Gardens, she began to hope that she might have succeeded. The snow had become heavy again, and she crept quietly into the small enclosed area through a narrow back gate, her footsteps muffled by the fresh snowfall.

From behind came a sound which could have been a foot crunching on ice. Felicity gasped. She looked round quickly for somewhere to hide – anywhere. There was only one possibility.

Two boys were building a snowman. As Felicity watched, they pushed a carrot into its inchoate features. They laughed and scrabbled in the snow raising flurries of flakes.

Quickly, Felicity ran to take shelter behind the snowman, standing so close she could feel the cold of its back. She would rather the children did not see her – she would rather that no one saw her. If her pursuer entered the gardens by the same approach as she had herself, then he would see only the boys and the snowman. All she need do was wait until Madame Vastra arrived .

But it was not to be.

For the man in the top hat came into Ranskill Gardens by a different route. He stood in the shadows by the back wall, watching the boys play. Watching the woman he had pursued standing in plain sight, ignorant of his presence. All he needed was a distraction.

It came in the form of the fireworks display. The boys turned to watch, their attention on the light-show, their ears assailed by the crack and thunder of distant explosions. So much so that a single gunshot echoing round the gardens was lost in the cacophony.

The bullet from the man's revolver struck Felicity in the centre of the back. It went right through her, penetrating and destroying her heart in an instant before traversing the soft body of the snowman and then embedding itself in the frozen ground nearby.

The force of the impact drove Felicity forwards with such violence that she was pressed into the snowman. Her body crashed through, almost to the other side. Blood wept from her gaping chest wound, through her coat, into the snow.

And in moments, as the two boys stood in awestruck horror, one with Felicity's blood staining his index finger, the weight of her body collapsed the fragile façade of the snowman, and she fell lifeless to the ground.

'So the murderer was the man Harry saw,' Jenny said.

Vastra nodded. 'That's why he wants Harry – to be rid of any possible witnesses.'

'Then we must defend the boy,' Strax decided. 'And the best form of defence is attack. I suggest a three-pronged assault on the villain's stronghold with ground forces. Shall I break out the heavy weapons?'

'We don't even know who this man is, let alone where he's taken Harry,' Jenny chided.

'Then we must begin surveillance on all possible suspects. Everyone who wears a dark coat and a top hat must be accounted for.'

'In London?' Jenny said. 'How many men do you think that would be?'

'There is only one that matters.'

'But we don't know which.'

'I think we do, actually,' Vastra told them. 'Remember what the policeman said.'

'Able Hecklington,' Jenny recalled. 'You think it was him?'

'I think,' Vastra said, 'that it would be impolite not to ask.'

A short way across London, the subject of these deliberations, Mister Able Hecklington, stood on a gantry high above the floor of his largest foundry. He looked down at the furnace below. A vast metal cauldron, it swirled with smoke so thick that it seemed to obscure the fire that produced it. A roiling mass of fog spilled over the edges and out across the foundry floor.

Hanging above the cauldron was a metal frame in the shape of a man – a cage. But the figure inside was smaller than a man. Strapped to the metal frame, Harry could barely turn his head to see Hecklington standing watching with satisfaction. Beside the man stood a smaller figure – Jim. The boy's face was pale, as if he only now began to understand what he had done. Or perhaps, what he had escaped by sacrificing his friend instead.

With the metallic clank of heavy chains, the cage containing Harry began slowly to descend. The smoke in the cauldron clawed at the air above, as if it was reaching out for the boy, beckoning for him to join it. Hungry for his company.

The Sixth Chapter

*In which a daring rescue
is attempted...*

The fog thickened as they approached the foundry
on foot. It hung in the air like a living thing.
Smoke from the vast brick chimneys added to the
coagulating sky.

'Hecklington owns many such facilities,' Strax
said. 'They could all be adapted for the production
of armaments with minimal disruption. How do we
know that this is where he has taken the boy?'

'It's the largest,' Jenny said.

'And more to the point,' Vastra commented, 'Miss
Felicity Gregson's house backs onto it. Whatever she
was bringing to show me, whatever story she had to
tell, it originated here.'

They made their wary way to a side door set in a
shadowy area close to the back of the foundry.

Vastra's sword was slung over her shoulder in a
scabbard especially designed for the purpose. Jenny
held a robust wooden pole, favoured by the oriental

masters of various martial disciplines. Strax had brought no weapon but himself, which was by any measure weapon enough.

'There may not be time,' Strax said, 'to conduct a full surveillance regime according to prescribed regulations in order to formulate a coherent strategy of the best method to effect entry.'

'That is true,' Madame Vastra agreed. 'So I suggest you simply break down this door.'

Strax flexed his hands, cracking all six sets of knuckles. 'My pleasure.' He adjusted his necktie.

Then, head down, he ran straight at the heavy wooden door. With a singularly unchromatic crunch, the apex of Strax's cranium connected with the door. The wood splintered, but did not break. Strax withdrew his head, and inspected the damage he had inflicted.

'Apologies,' he said. 'I shall need a longer run-up.'

Under the second onslaught, the door exploded inwards in a blizzard of splinters and shards, Strax in the very midst of the maelstrom. Close on his heels came Jenny and Madame Vastra herself. Each of the women had their weapons held ready.

The foundry was vast, not being delimited by internal walls or partitions. Smoke-darkened brick chimneys rose from huge furnaces to disappear into the shadowy limits of the roof space and thence up and out into the London air. Wrought iron gantries and walkways criss-crossed the area in a web of metal.

Central to the space was an enormous vat, shaped

like a witch's cauldron but immensely bigger. Smoke poured over the top of it like fog, falling towards the ground. It hugged the flagstoned floor, curling into every nook and cranny of the foundry. Jenny felt it catching at the back of her throat. Strax batted it away with the back of his tri-digital hand as one might an irksome fly.

Madame Vastra took in the scene at a glance. Through reptilian eyes well adjusted for seeing into darkness and shadow, she saw the metal cage above the roiling cauldron. She recognised the writhing form of the boy Harry as he was lowered, inch by inch, towards the smoking receptacle.

And above, watching and laughing, she saw the dark figure of Able Hecklington, who, at the same moment, turned slightly and saw Vastra and her compatriots.

Hecklington did not call out or gesture. But somehow, evidently, an order was given. In a moment, half a dozen men of the roughest and most uncouth variety appeared from the shadows around the cauldron, materialising as it were out of the drifting smoke. They were armed with cudgels and knives.

Vastra recognised two of the thugs as those self-same ruffians who had accosted Harry earlier. One of the two carried a revolver, which he raised to take aim at Strax.

This was something of a mistake. Despite his bulk, Strax could move quickly when the need arose. Arise it did, as the business end of the weapon pointed towards him. With a chilling, if unimaginative, Sontaran battle cry, he charged at his unfortunate opponent.

Again, the crown of Strax's head became a blunt instrument to be reckoned with. This time, the impact was immediately succeeded by a swift blow from the right arm. Kept straight and rigid, this was every bit as effective. The gun fell to the floor and its erstwhile owner was propelled at speed across the foundry.

The second of the returning ruffians backed away from Strax. But he lacked the velocity necessary to escape a similar blow that sent him stumbling to join his unconscious compatriot in a similar state of oblivion.

The other attackers should have fared no better against their apparently less brutal adversaries. Jenny and her mistress parried every blow from cudgel and every thrust from blade with pole and sword in a swirling blur of practised motion.

Had their attackers been made of more substantial stuff, they would have been felled in an instant.

But to the women's surprise and horror, their weapons cut right *through* the ruffians. It was as if the men were as insubstantial as the London smog. Where Vastra cut, a line of misty haze was all there was to show for even the most palpable hit. When Jenny thrust, what poured from the inflicted wound was not blood, but smoke!

'Strax!' Vastra shouted as she and Jenny fought back to back.

The two more substantial ruffians had regained some semblance of sense and were closing in on Strax, albeit rather cautiously. Strax paused in mid blow. 'Ma'am.' He turned, elbowing aside the nearest assailant in the same abrupt movement.

Vastra held the sword in one hand as she pointed to the cage descending from above. 'See to the boy!'

Where there had been two slowly recovering ruffians in front of Strax, suddenly there were none. Skittled away like ninepins, they rolled and stumbled aside as Strax hurried towards the huge cauldron. As he went, he scooped up the fallen revolver. His stubby fingers were too large to fit through the trigger guard, so with a grunt of irritation, he snapped it off.

The metal cage was attached by chains to a large cogwheel set in the wall of the foundry. With each movement of the wheel, the cage jerked down – another link of chain for every notch of the wheel. It was close enough in design to an ancient Sontaran instrument of torture that Strax understood the mechanism in a moment.

Another thing he understood with that inherent instinct bred into all Sontarans even before they are hatched, was weaponry – no matter how primitive by his own standards. He raised and fired the revolver as he was moving.

The bullet shattered through one of the chains holding the cage. Harry gave a startled cry as the cage swung violently. A second shot made short work of another chain, and Harry cried out again as the cage up-ended.

But still it was lowering slowly towards the smoking cauldron. Strax thrust the revolver into the inside pocket of his jacket for possible – or rather, probable – future use. He barrelled across the foundry towards the cauldron. The two chains that Strax had shot apart hung down from the cage, swinging back and forth. One of them dipped into the foggy cauldron.

The other swung wide of the lip. Strax took a running jump and caught hold of it. As he landed again, he dragged the chain. Harry stared down at him, eyes wide with fear as the cage fell another notch closer to the cauldron. The smoke curled up, clawing at him, stinging his eyes.

Below, Strax dragged the chain – and with it the cage above – away from the cauldron's edge. The cage clanged against the edge of the cauldron, but settled finally on the floor beside Strax.

Smoke was now pouring more abundantly from the cauldron, and Strax lost no time in breaking open the catches on the cage and the chains that held Harry's wrists and ankles. He heaved the grateful boy over his shoulder and marched off back through the smoke.

Vastra and Jenny were fighting a fierce rearguard action against the ruffians. They had no hope or way of winning against opponents who could withstand the most serious wounds. As soon as the sword cut through them, or the pole jabbed into them, the men healed and re-joined the fray.

But with Strax's appearance, marching out of

the swirling misty smoke towards them, Vastra and Jenny redoubled their efforts. Pausing only to hurl aside several of the attackers, Strax strode to the shattered doorway, and then out into the foggy night. Vastra and Jenny each made a final thrust, then turned and ran after Strax.

From his vantage point on the gantry above, Able Hecklington watched angrily as the intruders made good their escape.

'Boy!' he hissed.

Cowering behind him, Jim hardly dared to answer.

'We needed his form to infiltrate our enemies' lair. Instead they have found us. But perhaps all is not lost. You – boy – come here!' Hecklington roared.

Hesitantly, fearing the worst, Jim stumbled over to join Hecklington at the edge of the gantry. The man was leaning heavily on the side rail, looking down into the cauldron of boiling smoke below. He gestured for Jim to look also.

Jim leaned out, peering down. The smoke curled and swam like a living thing. It seemed thicker and darker by the moment.

'You see that?' Hecklington said. His voice was calmer now, quieter, almost like a father pointing out some interesting architectural feature to an eager son. 'You see the way the smoke beckons, how it coalesces and congeals?'

Jim nodded. 'Yes, sir,' he murmured.

Hecklington nodded. He clapped his hand

appreciatively to Jim's back. 'Then take a closer look.' His voice was a sudden snarl as he grabbed the back of Jim's jacket, lifted him bodily, and flung him over the rail.

The boy crashed down into the smoke below. As he fell, his last thoughts were that the patches of darkness in the smoke made it look like a face, the mouth gaping wide to welcome him. And that the sound of the air whistling past him was like the laughter of the most fiendish devil in hell.

The Seventh Chapter

*In which it seems the world
may soon come to an end...*

Madame Vastra and the others made their return
to Paternoster Row by a circumspect route. Strax in
particular was keen to intercept any individual he
suspected might be following and forcibly remove
a variety of their limbs and appendages. But Jenny
prevailed upon him that most of the people he singled
out were merely walking past. Given the lateness of
the hour there were, thankfully, not many.

'What about him?' Strax said, pointing to a figure
shambling slowly along on the opposite pavement.

'That old lady is selling lucky heather, and she's
heading in a different direction so she's unlikely to
be following us.'

'She could be bluffing. And who is this Lucky
Heather anyway?'

'It's heather – it's a plant not a person. It's
supposed to be lucky.'

'Not if I catch her, it won't be.'

'Strax,' Vastra said simply. 'No.'

Harry was in a daze for much of the journey. He felt he was living through a dream – a nightmare. It was an effort to put one foot in front of another. Wherever he looked, the gathering gloom of the London smog reminded him of the smoke in the cauldron below him as he was lowered down in his cage.

It was well into the night by the time they arrived back at Paternoster Row. Jenny sat Harry down before the fire in the drawing room, then withdrew to make a pot of tea. It took a while, and a lot of tea, but finally Harry felt recovered enough to recount his adventures.

He told them how Jim had found him in the carriage, and lured him to Able Hecklington.

'He wanted both possible witnesses taken care of,' Vastra said. 'I'm afraid your friend Jim will suffer a similar fate. He was merely postponing the inevitable.'

'He ain't my friend,' Harry said. 'Not no more, he ain't.'

Strax leaned across to Jenny. 'At what age do these cubs become grammatical?' he demanded.

'Depends,' she told him. 'At what age do Sontarans become pacifists?'

'Did he tell you anything of his plans?' Vastra was asking Harry.

The boy shook his head. 'Not really. But I did overhear him talking to Jim and to some of the other men. Like sort of boasting he was, about how everything was going according to plan.'

'What plan?' Strax asked. 'He has a strategy? Or is this merely tactical thinking at a preliminary stage of military operations?'

'Eh?'

'Ignore him,' Jenny whispered. Louder she said: 'Just tell us what you know. Anything might help, anything at all.'

Harry struggled to recall what he had overheard. He had been scared – more scared than he could ever remember, and Harry had already been through a lot in his short life.

'He talked a lot about "the Smoke".'

'The smoke? The smoke in that cauldron?' Jenny wondered.

'He said it like it was a living thing. He talked about meeting it, said he had come to an understanding with it.'

'Did he explain this Smoke's stratagem?' Strax asked.

'No. But he did say...' Harry's eyes widened as he remembered what he had heard. 'He said the Smoke would consume the world.'

Strax gave a snort of impatience. 'This tells us nothing. It makes no sense.'

'On the contrary,' Madame Vastra told him, 'it fits entirely with what I already know.'

They all turned towards the Lizard Woman.

'And what is that, Ma'am?' Jenny asked.

Madame Vastra's face was lit by the flickering red of the firelight as she told them her story. 'Several days ago, Miss Felicity Gregson contacted me in my capacity as the Great Detective. She was concerned about something that she had seen. A light, falling from the sky trailing smoke and fire. It came down behind her house, in the grounds of what we now know to be Mister Able Hecklington's foundry.'

'An invasion spearhead,' Strax said. 'Perhaps the first craft of many. The primitives of this planet should arm themselves ready for the assault.'

'Perhaps,' Vastra said. 'But moving on... Miss Gregson said that whatever had come down split open when it hit the ground. Smoke spilled out of it. She had something she wished me to see, though she was a little vague about what. I got the impression that she felt I would dismiss her story until I saw what she had. And perhaps I would have done. She referred to it as "evidence".'

'We had no other reports of anything falling to Earth in that area,' Jenny said.

'The other thing Miss Gregson told me, was that when she went back out into her garden the next morning, there was no sign of whatever had fallen. As if it had all been cleared away in the night.'

'By Hecklington,' Strax said.

'It seems likely. More than likely.'

'But what did she find?' Harry asked. 'What was she bringing to show you? She didn't have nothing with her when she fell dead out of our snowman.'

Strax leaned forward, about to speak.

But Jenny intervened. 'When he says "she didn't have nothing" he means that she *did* have nothing.'

'Ah!' Strax slapped his fist into his open palm. 'I understand – it is a *code*. Good, boy – very good. I shall give the impression that I don't not know what you ain't talking about.'

Vastra sighed. 'Thank you, Strax. But the question remains – what was the "evidence" that Miss Felicity Gregson was bringing to show me, and where is it now?'

'The police found nothing of interest,' Jenny said. 'That constable would have told me, I'm sure.'

'Then the murderer, Hecklington, took it,' Strax decided. 'The murder may have been in the nature of a recovery operation.'

'Tell us again what happened when you found the body,' Vastra said to Harry. 'We now know how she came to be inside your snowman.' She held up a gloved hand to stay Harry's immediate and vocal curiosity. 'I will explain in a moment, but first – tell us again what you saw.'

Harry's brow was creased with concentration as he tried to bring back an image of the moment. 'I'm trying to remember her hands,' he explained. 'When she fell, she had them in front of her. I thought it was like she was praying – making her peace with God.' He swallowed at the thought.

'Her hands were together, thus?' Vastra asked. She held her flattened palms together in front of her in demonstration.

'More like this, I think.' Harry clasped his own hands together more loosely by way of demonstration.

'She was holding something,' Jenny realised. 'Holding it tight between her hands.'

'But the police found nothing,' Vastra reminded her.

'The muscles would have relaxed when she fell, as the life ebbed from them,' Strax said. 'Her grip on the object would not be maintained.'

'She fell into the remains of the snowman.' Vastra's eyes were glittering in the firelight as she leaped to her feet. 'It would have been under her body, whatever it was. Pushed into the snow on the ground, just as she was propelled into the snowman itself.'

Jenny nodded, excited. 'We don't know what it is – but it might still be there!'

The Eighth Chapter

*In which the monstrous apparition
is revealed...*

Unable to keep his eyes open any longer, Harry fell into a deep sleep. Despite his fears and experiences, he seemed peacefully oblivious to reality. Strax carried him – surprisingly gently – upstairs to one of the many spare rooms in Vastra's large town house.

Also feeling the effects of a long day, Jenny agreed to stay with Harry. She settled down in a small armchair close to the boy's bed.

'We will lock up as we go,' Vastra assured her maidservant and friend.

'Allow no one access unless they know the pass code,' Strax instructed.

'What is the pass code?' Jenny asked.

Strax opened his mouth to reply, then closed it again. 'Allow no one access,' he decided.

'Is that the code, or another instruction?' Jenny asked, suppressing a tired smile.

'Children,' Vastra chided gently. 'Come, Strax, we have work to do.'

It was the darkest time of night as Strax and Vastra ventured forth from Paternoster Row. Vastra eschewed the carriage as she wanted time to think. The cool night air cleared her head, and there was once again a flurry of snow.

Strax stomped along beside her. Every seventeen steps, he turned in a full circle to check they were not being observed. Satisfied that they were not, he then resumed his stomp.

As they arrived again at Ranskill Gardens, the moon appeared from behind the clouds though the snow was still falling. Strax glared up at the moon, as if daring it to stay visible, looking down at them. Within a few moments, clouds had once more obscured its crescent-face, and Strax breathed a satisfied sigh as if he had just won a staring competition.

Vastra strode over to the remains of the boys' snowman. It was now little more than an uneven pile of snow. More had fallen over the top, further obscuring the shape and location.

'Here, Strax, help me.'

She brushed away the top layer of snow with her gloved hand. More snow fell to take its place, but she brushed that aside also. Strax crouched beside her, and she motioned for him to scrape more of the snow.

'But carefully. We do not know what may lie beneath.'

'A heat ray would complete the task more efficiently,' Strax said.

'And it might damage whatever is hidden here. This is best.'

They continued to feel their way down through the snow until Vastra felt the frozen ground beneath. She sighed with disappointment.

'There's nothing here.'

'No,' Strax agreed. 'Would you care for a toffee?'

Vastra shook her reptilian head, still staring down at the hole they had so unproductively scraped in the snow. 'Not at the moment, thank you, Str—'

She broke off, turning to look up at Strax standing behind her.

'A *toffee*?'

Strax held up a battered tin. 'I found this. It says "Lovelock's Famous Treacle Toffee" in human writing, look.' He pointed with his other hand to the faded printing on the rusty surface. '"Would you care for a toffee? Only if it's Lovelock's. The Original and Still the Best".' He hesitated a moment before asking: 'What is toffee?'

'Don't open it!' Vastra called, getting quickly back to her feet and taking the tin from Strax.

'Toffee is a weapon?'

'In this case, that is entirely possible,' Vastra agreed. 'Show me where you found this.'

Strax indicated an area where the snow had been wiped away, in close proximity to where Vastra had herself been searching. More snow was already settling and obscuring the impression.

'Strax,' she said slowly, 'what do you think we were looking for?'

Strax considered.

'It is not a trick question,' Vastra told him after a long pause.

'We were looking for whatever the Felicity human was holding.'

'Which was?'

'I… don't… know…'

'No, none of us knows.'

Strax looked relieved at this revelation.

'So,' Madame Vastra continued, 'is it not possible that she was holding a toffee tin?'

Strax's eyes widened slightly and he took an inadvertent step backwards, crushing a post-nasal carrot.

'A toffee tin into which she had perhaps placed whatever evidence it was that she wished to bring to me?'

Strax pointed dumbly at the tin Vastra was holding, his lower lip shaking slightly in an unformed question.

'Indeed,' Vastra agreed. 'I suggest that as the snow shows no sign of letting up, we return to Paternoster Row and open the tin under controlled conditions.'

This Strax could understand. He strode ahead of his mistress. 'I shall provide a security escort for the evidence toffee. Once safely locked inside Paternoster Row, I shall instigate an exclusion zone and organise frequent patrols as well as establishing an observation station and surveillance regime.'

'You know,' Vastra said as she followed her henchman, 'for once you may not be overreacting. I have a feeling whatever is inside this tin will require treating with the utmost caution.'

She brushed a thin layer of snow from its surface. As if in reply, the tin in her hands vibrated and shook – for all the world like something inside was trying to force off the lid…

The glass tank was airtight. Through two holes in the sides, rubberised gloves reached inside, the wrists sealed to the glass. Since the containment vessel had been designed and manufactured specifically for members of the race of which the troll-like Strax was a member, it was Strax whose bifurcated hands were thrust into the gloves.

Inside the tank lay the rusty toffee tin recovered from the scene of the murder of Felicity Gregson. Carefully, Strax lifted the tin in one large hand. With the other he grasped the lid. Gently he eased it off the main body and lifted it clear.

Vastra, Jenny, and Harry all peered closely through the glass.

'There's nothing in it,' Harry proclaimed, echoing Jenny's thoughts.

'No – there is something,' Vastra breathed.

It was thin and ethereal – as insubstantial as mist, as inchoate as the London fog itself. A curl of smoke licked out of the tin, as if exploring the surrounding air. It lifted lazily from the tin, thinning and drifting across the tank.

'Is that it?' Strax asked. 'Not much of an enemy. A good sneeze would see that off. Not,' he added, 'like Moonites!'

'What are Moonites?' Harry asked.

'A figment of whatever Strax has instead of imagination,' Jenny told him.

'The Ancient Enemy,' Strax proclaimed.

'I thought that was the Rutan Host,' Vastra said.

'I believe the two are in league.' Strax nodded. 'A formidable alliance.'

'It looks like smoke,' Harry said. 'Like that smoke they tried to lower me into. With a face, and everything.'

'A face?' Vastra turned back to the glass tank.

Jenny gasped. Strax reached for a weapon he did not have.

In the tank, the smoke had indeed drifted into a vague, round shape. Darker patches might have been eyes. A slash of emptiness could be a mouth.

'What do we do with it?' Jenny asked.

But her words were interrupted by the jangling of a distant bell.

'Keep it in there, Strax,' Vastra said. 'And Jenny – see who's at the door.'

Harry followed Jenny. He was not at all interested in who might be calling, but he wanted to get as far from the smoke creature as he could. He trusted and liked Jenny, so he felt safer close to her. He stood at the back of the hall, in the shadow of the staircase, and watched her open the door.

Then in a moment, he was running forwards – towards the visitor now framed in the entrance.

'Jim!' he exclaimed, for it was indeed his friend who stood on the threshold. He might have betrayed Harry, but that was out of fear which Harry understood and forgave. He was happy just to see the boy alive and safe.

Except...

As Harry reached the doorway, he saw what Jenny had already noticed – and which had frozen her momentarily into inaction. He shared her feelings of surprise and dread.

For the boy Jim's eyes were devoid of pupils. Instead a pale, foggy discolouration drifted across the iris. He raised a hand, and wisps of smoke curled out from the ends of his cuffs. More smoke was escaping from the gap between his neck and the loose collar of his grubby shirt.

When Jim opened his mouth to speak, it emitted a cloud of smoke, like an expulsion of steam.

'It's all right,' the boy said, his voice gravel-rough and entirely without inflection. His whole form was now wreathed in smoke. 'I escaped. Please let me in.'

The Ninth Chapter

*In which Paternoster Row is besieged
by the Devil in the Smoke...*

'Please let me in,' Jim said again. The smoke around him seemed to mingle with the gathering fog.

The sound of the boy's inhuman voice shocked Jenny into action. 'Not bloomin' likely!' she told him, and slammed the front door shut. She turned the key in the lock and shot the bolts.

Alerted by the sound of the door slamming, Vastra was almost immediately on the scene. Strax strode purposefully after her.

'It's Jim,' Harry explained, breathless and frightened. 'He's gone peculiar. Like his insides are full of smoke or something.'

'Or something,' Jenny agreed.

'Stand back from the door,' Strax instructed.

'Don't do anything stupid, Strax,' Jenny said.

'No,' Vastra said, 'he's right – stand back from the door now!'

As Jenny obeyed the instructions of her mistress

and hurried back down the hallway, they could all see it. The faintest curls of smoke were edging round the door frame. More forced its way through the letterbox. It gathered close to the door, thickening as more of the grotesque miasma found its way inside.

'Strax,' Vastra said, 'where is the best place in the house to defend?'

'Not the drawing room,' Jenny said, checking.

Smoke was forcing its way round the sash windows and puffing out from behind the curtains. As Jenny watched, more smoke wafted out of the fireplace and drifted across the room towards her.

She closed the door quickly. 'It's coming down the chimney!'

'Then an internal chamber,' Strax suggested. 'Where there are no windows or outside openings. I suggest the room where we set up the isolation tank.'

'No windows in there,' Vastra agreed.

'No chimney, neither,' Jenny added.

They were already moving, hurrying back to the room they had so recently vacated. Jenny bundled young Harry ahead of her.

Behind them, smoke continued to gather in the hallway. It thickened and merged, hardening into an outline – a silhouette within which the smoke drifted and pulsed...

But it was not only from the front of the house that the smoke was mounting its assault. It seeped in round windows and outside doors. It poured down chimneys and cascaded out through fireplaces. By the time Vastra and her companions reached the room that was their destination, a pall of smoke hung in the air before them. More rolled along low to the ground, like mist coming off a river.

The smoke thickened, forming shapes – tendrils that reached out to clutch at Vastra and the others. Ethereal hands clawed at the air. Faces leered up from the rolling fog.

'Don't breathe it in,' Vastra ordered. 'We have to get through it – close your eyes, hold your breath, and run!'

'I shall go last,' Strax said.

'More heroics?' Jenny chided.

'Any of you that falter, I will assist. I shall carry you if I have to.'

'Thank you,' Jenny said, moved by his uncharacteristic concern.

'And anyone infected by this smoke,' Strax went on, 'I will tear to pieces. For their own good, of course.'

No one ventured thanks for this. They all ran, eyes closed, breath held, for the door through which they hoped and prayed safety lay. The smoke clutched and tore at them. It dragged claws through Harry's hair and grabbed at Jenny. It closed about Vastra and threw itself at Strax.

But they stumbled onwards, and somehow managed to burst through the foggy barrier and out the other side.

Vastra fumbled for the handle, threw the door wide. They tumbled inside and Strax pushed the door shut behind them. He slammed it so hard that it was forced into the frame, sealing the edges tight.

'That should keep the smoke out,' Jenny said.

But Harry was not so sure. With the perception of youth, he pointed out her error: 'Keyhole!'

Sure enough, a wisp of smoke was already curling through this narrow aperture. Strax placed his hand over the keyhole, cutting off access for the nebulous creature.

'I shall stand here while you all escape,' he declared.

'Escape how?' Vastra asked. 'There are no other doors and no windows. That is why we came here.'

Strax gave a grunt that might have been understanding or disagreement. 'There is a way. One which I prepared a while ago for such an eventuality.'

'You thought we'd be besieged in here by a smoke demon?' Jenny said. 'That's foresight.'

'An escape route is always valuable. Forward planning is essential. There is only one small problem.'

'Which is?'

'*I* shall have to effect the escape. Only my structure is of sufficient resilience and potency. I cannot perform this task *and* keep my finger over the keyhole.'

'We have no need of escape yet,' Vastra told him.

She was holding a copy of *The Times*, and as the others watched she shredded it into strips with her claws. Jenny realised at once her mistress's purpose. While the door was tight in its frame, there was still a small gap beneath. Smoke was seeping through – a thin mist for the moment, but soon it would thicken and coagulate.

With Harry's help, Jenny and Vastra twisted the strips of paper and pushed them into the gap. Harry took another strip and gestured for Strax to move his hand. As soon as the troll-like creature obliged, he forced his twist of paper into the keyhole, thereby obstructing it entirely.

'Now what?' Jenny asked.

'Now we wait,' Vastra said. 'That smoke creature is here for a purpose. I imagine we shall soon discover what the purpose is.'

'It's purpose is assault,' Strax told her. 'It means to kill us all.'

'Perhaps – but why?'

'We know about it,' Jenny said. 'Perhaps that's enough?'

They did not have long to wait to find out. Jim's voice, although they all knew it no longer emanated from Jim, came to them through the door – muffled and uninflected.

'You cannot escape,' the voice said.

'You cannot get in,' Vastra called back through the door. 'What do you want?'

'To be complete,' came the level reply.

'Complete? What's it mean?' Harry asked.

Vastra walked over to the glass tank. The smoke inside swirled angrily round the open and empty toffee tin.

'Is this what it wants?' she wondered aloud.

'Incomplete is painful,' the voice from beyond the door said. 'We must be whole if we are to grow and thicken and blot out the sun. We must be complete if we are to encircle and envelop this world and hold it in our grasp.'

'Good,' Strax said.

The others looked at him.

'Because,' he explained, 'this means we have a hostage.'

'Return the rest of us, and we shall let you go free,' the voice said.

'What guarantee do we have of that?' Vastra asked.

'You have… my word.'

'Not enough,' Strax snarled. 'We shall arrange a hostage exchange on our terms at a location and time of our choosing under controlled conditions according to the protocols of the Shadow Proclamation.'

There was a pause, as if the smoke was considering.

'If we give them back the rest of this stuff, they're going to destroy the world!' Jenny pointed out.

'We can at least play for time,' Vastra said.

The answer to this came from within the room, a quiet whisper in the voice of the ill-fated Jim:

'You have no time left.'

The smoke in the glass tank was a face – Jim's face, staring out at them. The foggy mouth twisted into a ghastly smile. Then the whole visage seemed to burst apart into mist – mist that at once reformed in the shape of a fist.

The fist punched forwards, shattering the side of the tank. Fragments of glass flew across the room, whipping past Harry's face. Smoke poured out from the tank, like water cascading through the broken glass. Vastra and the others watched in horror as the smoke congealed before them into the sinister shape of Able Hecklington.

The Tenth Chapter

*In which our heroes
are trapped beneath glass...*

As the fearsome creature of fog was still coalescing before them, Vastra shouted: 'I think it is time for that escape route you promised us, Strax.'

'There is no way out,' the creature said. Its laughter echoed off the oak panelling that lined the unbroken walls.

The self-same panelling that Strax, without need for further instruction, ran straight towards. He lowered his massive shoulders and crashed into a wooden section. There was an echoing crunch, accompanied by a grunt of pain from Strax, who rebounded and stumbled backwards.

'Sorry,' he gasped. 'Wrong panel.'

Strax reoriented himself, and ran again at the wall. This time when he hurled himself at an oaken panel, the wood exploded in a shower of splinters, revealing a troll-shaped hole, with Strax the other side.

The foggy form of Hecklington gave a shout of displeasure as Vastra ushered first Harry and then Jenny through the penetrated panel. Once they were safe, she dived after them.

Hecklington dissolved into a stream of mist, billowing after its prey.

On the other side of the panel was a narrow corridor, which led to the scullery. The corridor and scullery were mercifully free of smoke, which Vastra surmised had gathered in its entirety outside the door of the room they had so recently vacated. Egress via wall was not an option it had seriously considered.

But now the smoke was most definitely in pursuit. Strax hurried through the scullery, barging through the outer door, and holding it open for the others to exit. Then he turned back to face the oncoming smoke. It spread across the scullery like a lethal blanket, ready to smother him. Hecklington's face stared out malevolently from the middle of this wall of smoke.

'Retreat is not an option for Sontarans,' Strax declared, bracing himself for the inevitable. 'It will be a glorious death.'

Vastra's face appeared back through the door. 'We are not retreating. We are regrouping.'

Strax considered this. The smoke surged forwards.

Strax nodded. 'That is permitted.' He slammed the door on the smoke. 'I suggest we regroup in the carriage. Rapidly.'

*

Remembering his discomfort when first travelling in the carriage, Harry quickly climbed up beside Strax to sit on the driver's box.

Strax turned to glare at him. Then his mouth and nose twitched slightly, and he nodded. 'Welcome aboard, boy.'

As soon as Vastra and Jenny were inside and the doors closed, Strax cracked the reins and the horses leaped forwards.

A pall of smoke emanated from the yard behind them as the carriage rattled towards the main road. But they were not free of it yet. Out in Paternoster Row, the smoggy night hardened into a shape before the carriage.

'Look out!' Harry yelled.

But Strax held firm to the reins, goading the horses onwards.

The fog was coagulating, rushing inwards to fill the silhouette of Hecklington – complete with top hat – in the middle of the roadway. He held up a smoking hand to stop them, mist streaming from his fingers.

But Strax was not deterred. The carriage ploughed right into the figure, scattering Hecklington's form as if he were made of dust. Fog curled round the wheels, blown aside by the passage of the vehicle, yet already clotting again behind it. This time the figure it formed faced the other way – watching the carriage depart into the night.

Inside the conveyance, Vastra and Jenny discussed

what they had learned. Vastra was of the opinion that they must possess some clue to the weaknesses of the creature made of smoke – otherwise why would it continue to pursue them even after recovering it vestigial components?

'Perhaps it's just angry with us, Ma'am,' Jenny ventured. 'Or it don't want no one to know what it's up to.'

Vastra rapped on the ceiling of the carriage with the hilt of her sword. 'Strax, drive past Hecklington's foundry. We may see some clue there.'

Strax's face appeared upside down outside the carriage window. 'Clue to what?'

'The weaknesses of our enemy.'

'Ah! Agreed.'

'Is it following us?' Jenny asked.

The upside-down face disappeared for a moment. 'Yes,' it said when it returned. 'Excuse me, I surmise that speed is needed.' It went again.

The carriage sped through the night. Behind it a huge cloud of foggy smoke rolled along the street. Anyone who stepped into its path was enveloped in the choking mist, coughing and gasping for air, left dead on the pavement as the smoke rolled onwards after its quarry.

'More smoke!' Strax called out as they approached the foundry.

'It's like it's making the stuff,' Harry said.

The foundry's chimneys were belching dark clouds into the air, blotting out the moon. Smoke was also pouring from the windows and doorways of Hecklington's foundry, rolling and merging, coming together into a huge face that stared down at the carriage. Able Hecklington's face. The mouth snarled open, blowing out a great breath of fog – the whole monstrous visage projected out of its own mouth at the carriage.

Strax pulled hard on the reins. The horses wheeled, and the carriage leaned suddenly sideways, somehow finding a narrow side alley. Sparks flew from the brick walls on either side as the carriage scraped through. Smoke poured after it.

'I fear the entire creature is now after us,' Strax called into the carriage. 'Apologies. I shall continue to regroup at speed.'

Another sharp turn, and then another. But still the smoke rolled after them. Harry had lost track of where they were until the carriage sped between ornate iron gates and onto a narrow path. It lurched down a grassy incline, off the road. Ahead of them, a vast glass structure glittered in the cold moonlight.

'The Crystal Palace!' Harry realised.

'It looks like a big greenhouse,' Strax said, unimpressed.

But Harry was staring in awe. The huge glass sides were coated with frost. Snow lay deep across the roof, blanketing the entire vast structure with white. More snow was starting to fall now, thickening even as the carriage lurched again on the uneven, snow-bound grass.

'I fear we may soon have to abandon this primitive transport,' Strax grumbled. 'It has no all-terrain setting.'

No sooner had he spoken than a wheel struck something hard embedded in the ground. One side of the carriage leaped into the air, crashing down so hard the wheel buckled under the weight. The carriage slewed sideways before coming to a halt, half buried in snow.

Harry tumbled off the driver's box, and plummeted into the thick snow drift. He surfaced, cold and shivering to find Strax assisting Vastra out of the side door of the carriage – which was now on its top. Jenny clambered after.

'Where's the smoke gone?' Jenny asked as she climbed down.

Strax turned to look. 'It was close behind us.'

Snow was settling on Vastra's face as she too looked. This seemed somewhat peculiar to Harry, but another thought was uppermost in his mind at this time.

'Is it something to do with the snow?' he asked. He had to raise his voice almost to a shout, as he was on the opposite side of the drifting bank of snow to where Jenny and Vastra had alighted and where Strax now stood.

'Explain!' Strax rasped.

Harry wasn't sure what he meant. He shrugged. 'The smoke thing could have snuffed out that Felicity woman. Instead Hecklington shot her. And it sent those men after me – why didn't it come itself? It was snowing both those times, and it's snowing now – maybe the smoke demon just doesn't like snow.'

'It was trapped, a portion of it at least, within the toffee tin,' Vastra said thoughtfully. 'I could feel it trying to escape, and from the way it smashed the glass it was certainly strong enough to force the lid from the tin.'

'Maybe it had to gather its strength, sort of build up to it,' Jenny said. 'And the snow stopped it. It doesn't like the cold, or the wet...'

'Or the combination of the two,' Vastra agreed.

'Which is a pity,' Strax said. 'Because the snow is stopping.'

The last few flakes twisted lazily down to settle on the ground. A cloud skittered across the moon. Yet, it seemed closer than the moon – far closer. And this was no ordinary cloud.

'It's the smoke!' Harry shouted. 'Let's get out of here.' He ran.

On the other side of the snowdrift, Vastra motioned for Strax to follow the boy. 'Keep him safe,' she ordered.

'But what about you?'

'Jenny and I will be fine. Now – go!'

The smoke was gathering speed. Fog and mist poured into it, swelling the cloud until it was a veritable wall of grey flowing across the park. And in the very midst of it, a huge face, as if Able Hecklington had been hewn from the fog itself and was visiting his fury upon them.

Vastra and Jenny backed away down the hill. Finally they turned and ran – heading for the only shelter available: the Crystal Palace.

At this hour, the great glasshouse was of course deserted. But a moment with a picklock enabled Jenny to gain access via a side door, and she and her mistress hurried inside.

Behind them, the smoke hurled itself at the glass, pressing against it like London smog, desperate to get in. Faces appeared and disappeared, each staring in, trying to observe where Jenny and Vastra had taken refuge.

The snow on the roof allowed a modicum of moonlight to penetrate, bathing the entire structure in an unearthly pale ambience.

As the smoke continued to press up against the walls, Vastra drew her sword. 'I fear we may have made what Strax might call a tactical error,' she said.

Looking around, Jenny could see her argument. The grey mist pressed in on the walls, enveloping the whole side of the building. If they tried to escape, it would come after them. But the Crystal Palace, magnificent feat of engineering though it was, could not exclude the smoke from every joint and opening. Already the ethereal creature was seeping through, gaining corporeality within the environs of glass.

Back to back, Vastra and Jenny stood in a side gallery of the great exhibition hall. Vastra raised her sword. Jenny adopted a fighting stance. Together they waited for the smoke to coalesce into their opponents – a dozen Hecklingtons, a score of Jims, ruffians without number, all composed of hazy nothing. All poised to attack.

The Final Chapter

*In which the monstrous creature
is finally dispelled...*

There was something close behind Harry. He could hear its footsteps pounding into the snow. Could see the moonlight shadow of its grotesque form outstripping his own as he ran. After the day's exertions, Harry was close to exhaustion. As the shadow's arms reached out towards his own dark silhouette against the snowy ground, he resigned himself to his unpleasant fate.

Then Strax's hands closed on his shoulders, and lifted him bodily.

'The human form tires too easily for sustained combat,' he said, not unsympathetically. 'I must carry you if we are to outrun – er, regroup from the smoke creature.'

Looking back over Strax's shoulder, Harry saw a grey face formed of mist pursuing them across the snowy park. The whole of the Crystal Palace was wreathed in the same insubstantial material – so much smoke it was as if the fires of hell itself had fuelled the apparition.

A line of trees materialised out of the hazy gloom ahead. At first they were vague, pencil-sketches of reality. Their upper branches, denuded of leaves since autumn, were laden instead with snow. Strax and Harry arrived at the trees just as the deadly grey mist reached them.

Foggy fingers lashed out, clawing at Harry, ripping him from Strax's grasp. He was flung sideways, lungs choking on the pungent smoke. Strax too was knocked forwards and crashed head first into the substantial trunk of an ancient oak tree.

With a bellow of triumph from its mighty mouth, the smoke plunged towards Harry. He landed on his back, staring up at a massive grey face, a grotesque parody of his friend Jim, bearing down on him. About to devour his very being.

Above that, vague and insubstantial through the smoke, he saw the top of the tree shiver in response to the impact of Strax on its lower regions. A trickle of snow fell from the topmost branches. It sprinkled down through the smoky mist, drilling tiny holes in the ersatz face and pattering onto Harry. Behind it, more snow dislodged by the first tiny trickle became a stream, dislodging still more until an avalanche of white tumbled from the heavily laden branches.

The smoke-face was almost upon Harry when the avalanche hit. It crashed down through the smoke, scattering it. The cry of triumph became a scream of rage, then pain. Then nothing. Silence.

Harry blinked the snow from his eyes to see Strax hauling himself to his feet nearby. The stocky manservant straightened his cravat, adjusted his cuffs, and held out a hand to pull Harry upright. His small, deep-set eyes glittered in the snowy moonlight. Of the smoke that had so nearly engulfed Harry, there was no sign.

'It seems you were right, young human. We have a weapon,' Strax proclaimed. 'Now we must find a way to deploy it.'

The smoke pressed in on all sides. Figures of fog, men of mist, multiple Hecklingtons and facets of Jim... All advanced on Jenny and Madame Vastra.

Vastra's sword cut through the figures, spilling smoke like blood that dripped and drifted across the enclosed space. Sharp steel shone in the snow-filtered moonlight.

Jenny's kicks and blows passed through the smoke creatures with barely any resistance. As the creatures closed in, they conjoined – flowing together into a coalescing mass of smoke, drifting ever closer, encircling Vastra and Jenny.

The smoke muffled noise just as it diffused light. But through it, Jenny could see Strax hammering on a glass wall. Beside him, Harry's frightened face was pressed close to the glass. Snow was falling round them, covering their shoulders as both gestured upwards.

'What do they mean?' Jenny asked.

Vastra turned, delivering a robust blow to the

nearest area of smoke. It scattered under the breeze of the impact, immediately reforming.

'It's snowing hard outside again. The smoke is all in here with us. Perhaps that is what they mean.'

'Doesn't help,' Jenny said, lashing out with one foot while twisting round on the heel of the other.

'If we defeat this creature here, we destroy it all,' Vastra said.

'How likely is that?'

The smoke was drifting ever closer. Its laughter echoed off the glass walls and roof.

Vastra looked up, towards the high ceiling. A covering of white pressed against the transparent roof, now blotting out the moonlight completely as it thickened in this latest snowfall.

'Perhaps there is a way,' Vastra breathed. 'And perhaps Strax and the boy have found it.'

Jenny paused before landing another blow. 'What must we do, Ma'am?'

'Be ready. Be in the right place. And wrap up warm.'

The glass was slippery and the metal struts that connected and held the individual panes in place were cold and damp. Strax went first, his large, strong hands gripping the strut tightly.

'Follow me,' he ordered.

It was easier said than done. But Harry persevered. He slipped back down a few inches for every foot he climbed. Hand over hand, reaching to any and every point of purchase.

Once, he fell. His hands slipped and he felt himself falling backwards. Then a three-fingered hand grabbed his arm and hoisted him back again. Strax made a grunting noise that seemed to encapsulate disappointment, then continued the slow, relentless journey upwards.

The snow was becoming a blizzard. Harry's face was so cold he had lost all feeling. His fingers were so numb he could scarcely hang on. The snow stung his eyes as he continually blinked it away. The air was white, and there was no way to see how far they had still to climb.

Through the glass, Harry saw the smoke drifting ever closer to Vastra and Jenny as they fought back with brave determination. But the grey wall pressed in ever closer...

Finally, as he thought he might freeze in position and be discovered as an iced statue of himself, Harry felt the top of the wall. Strax leaned back down to haul him up and over the guttering onto the glass roof.

'We must keep to the iron support beams,' Strax said. 'Follow in my footsteps, boy.'

Harry followed the improbable Wenceslas across the roof. The snow was deep and crisp and even, but the iced glass was slippery. When they reached the middle of this section of the roof, Strax crouched down and wiped away a small area of snow, clearing a vantage point from where they could look down into the Crystal Palace below.

The grey surrounded Vastra and Jenny. It was

almost touching them on all sides, slowly closing in as if savouring the moment. Strax tapped, with surprising moderation, on the glass. Far below, Vastra glanced up. She nodded.

'What now?' Harry asked.

'Since we lack a supply of scissor grenades, we shall wait until they are directly beneath us.'

'And then what?' Harry wondered through chattering teeth.

Strax's wide, thin mouth twisted into a smile. 'Then – we jump!'

'There they are,' Vastra said quietly to Jenny.

'We need to move,' Jenny said. 'About four yards to your left.'

'Better hold your breath. I'll count to three.'

'Let's hope Strax is ready.'

'He's a Sontaran,' Vastra said. 'If we're talking about a foolhardy but heroic gesture that could end in death and destruction, then he's always ready. The question is – are we?'

She counted to three.

Then Madame Vastra and Jenny hurled themselves at the smoke. It clawed at them, smothering them in a sudden oppression of suffocating fog. They struggled through, knowing that there was no way out – that their only hope was some distance above them.

Seeing their movement, Strax and Harry leaped off the metal crossbeam that bore their load. Harry's weight was slight, but added to the hefty bulk of

Strax and the persistent weight of the deep snow it was enough.

The glass roof cracked – a spider's web of fine lines shot out across the pane. The stress breached the metal stanchion to the next pane, and then on again to the one beyond that.

With an ear-splitting crack, the entire section of roof gave way.

Glass and snow crashed down. Vastra and Jenny were flung to the ground, turning away from the splinters of ice and glass. The world was a blizzard of grey and white. Harry's scream mingled with a guttural cry of: 'Sontar-Ha!'

The smoke creature, gathered for the final kill, was concentrated under the very point of collapse. The broken glass passed through it, making hardly an impact. But the snow was a different matter. It crushed down on the smoke, a sudden avalanche of white against the grey. The snow seemed almost to absorb the creature, damping it down. Grey seeped into white – diluted and dispelled.

For a few seconds, a face was apparent on the surface of the fallen snow. The face of the unfortunate Able Hecklington stared up at the broken roof, at the snow falling through and drifting into the Crystal Palace. The mouth formed a scream of pain and anger, of suffering and regret. But no sound emerged from the frozen lips, and in a moment, it was gone – drifted across as more snow fell.

The next break in the fallen snow was the tip of a sword, followed first by Madame Vastra, and then by Jenny Flint – coughing and spluttering, but laughing with relief.

Strax's head emerged from another part of the white drift. He looked about him, frowned, then ducked under the snow again. Only to re-emerge lifting young Harry clear of the freezing landscape.

The boy looked round in a daze, blinking ice from his eyes. He took in the huge snowfall now carpeting the floor of this whole area of the great glass edifice.

'I ain't sweeping this lot up,' he said. 'Though, mind you – it'd make a great snowman.'

Back at Paternoster Row, Harry once again enjoyed the warming ministrations of Jenny's soup. Even Strax risked a taste, though he muttered ominously about the greater efficacy of probic vent energising.

Vastra and Jenny sat together sipping tea.

'I s'pose it's back to the workhouse now?' Harry said at last. He had been summoning up the courage to say it for a while, knowing there could be but one answer.

'Alas there is insufficient room here for another guest,' Vastra said. She set down her tea cup on its saucer. 'And you might not take kindly to some of our other guests. Or they to you. But,' she went on, 'there may be other options.'

'You acquitted yourself well, young one,' Strax said. 'I shall make immediate enquiries about your suitability for enrolment in the Sontaran Greater Military Academy. What do you say to that?' He punctuated the question with a hearty slap on the back which propelled Harry almost into his soup bowl.

'Thank you,' the boy spluttered.

'Or you can go and work as a kitchen boy for my friend Mary,' Jenny said. 'She's housekeeper to a lord out near Lincoln. She could do with some help. And you can come back and visit us now and then.'

'Which would you prefer?' Madame Vastra asked.

Strax gave a snort of amusement. 'It is surely a very simple choice. One option is for a quiet life with honest work amongst other humans paying a living wage and with prospects of promotion within a distinguished household. The other...' He drew himself up to his full height and looked up at them, 'is the prospect of constant danger, fear and risk. No chance of ever seeing your friends again, or of making new ones. The knowledge that death waits around the next corner and you are unlikely to see the end of next week without at the very least a serious injury. A glorious alternative.'

'So which is it to be?' Vastra asked.

'Yes,' Jenny prompted, 'what do you think, Harry.'

Harry looked round at this strange triumvirate: the Lizard Woman, the Troll, and the Parlour Maid. Strax was right, he thought – it really was a very simple choice.

Outside, dawn was breaking over London. The city was waking up to a bright winter's morning. Cabs rattled through the streets; servants drew back curtains; shopkeepers unlocked their doors; and children impatient for Christmas played in the cold, soft snow…

The Girl Who Never Grew Up

An extract from
an interview in *Brooklyn Fayre*, 1969,
by Chrissie Allen

Gather round, you sugar lumps! Come here, you little jelly tots! For I've a golden ticket to a Fairy Castle and if you're very good little girls and boys I'll hide you in my skirts and we can all sneak in together. Come along! Hush now!

For years now, Amelia Williams has been throwing open the gates of Wonderland annually, chucking out a book, then slamming them shut again. But today, I've got a magical pass to her gingerbread house (Upper West Side, 3rd Floor).

I may be a little old to appreciate her books, but I've a bunch of nieces and nephews who assure me that the pen of Mrs Williams lays golden eggs.

So, what's the Queen of Faerieland like – is she sugar and spice and all things nice, or is she a right old Wicked Witch of the West? I have to say readers, a little from column A, a lot from column B.

For a princess whose mattresses must be stuffed with cash, she lives quite simply. The building she lives in could do with a sweep from a magic broomstick. When she opens the door, Amelia Williams looks bleary-eyed and a little startled. If you ask me, the night before she met me, she'd been at the bottle labelled 'Drink Me'.

'And you are...?' she begins. I'll tell you now, Queen Titania needs to have a few words with her Pixie Publicist. It's not a great first move. Her second isn't much better. I give my name and she blinks. 'Stenographer... Dressmaker... or the new Cleaner?'

I introduce myself, and her mouth manages a very pretty 'Oh.' A silence hangs between us.

'Sorry, I've only just woken up,' Sleepy Beauty proclaims. Which explains the dressing gown and the Medusa hair. We can all sympathise, can't we readers – we've all gone to bed late and merry, only to be woken up way too soon by a knock at the door. For most of us it's just the postmen. Sadly for Amelia Williams, it's *Brooklyn Fayre* come to do a profile.

It is at this point that Mr Williams steps in. He's quite a dashing figure, even in pyjamas. With the air of a man who spends a lot of his time smoothing things over, he offers me tea. Yes, he's the most British Brit you can imagine. He also insists on making me that height of English Cuisine, the Bacon Sandwich. Or, as he says, 'I don't know about you, but I'm dying for one.'

We sit in chairs in the living room, eating our sandwiches while Mrs Williams runs around in the bedroom, dressing loudly. Conversation with the husband is awkward, and punctuated by the occasional interjection from Mrs Williams that you certainly wouldn't hear coming from any of the characters in her books. Not even the famous *Night Thief of Ill-Harbour*.

I ask Mr Williams if he likes living in his wife's shadow. He shrugs. It's a good, well-oiled shrug. 'I'm used to it.'

I point out to him that he's made quite a name for himself in his own field. He might not write about magic wands, but he's cast quite a spell in the world of medicine. A bit of astute boosting of one drug over another, and a few quiet innovations in medical supplies. I tell him that my aunt praised his name every day when she was in hospital for her hip operation. The Williams Wonder Beds, apparently, more than live up to their name. He smiles, bashfully. I guess he even cleans his teeth bashfully. 'I, ah, trained as a nurse...' A hesitant little frown, and he mutters about the Spanish Civil War.

'Oh really?' I tell him. 'That's interesting. Sometimes you say it was during the Second World War–'

'That too...' His eyes are nervous.

'But weren't you already living in New York by then?'

Mr Williams looks surprisingly alarmed. Which is when Mrs Williams swishes in, the Damsel coming to the rescue of her White Knight in distress. 'There were a lot of wounded on the convoy boats,' she barks.

Mr Williams nods, and squeezes his wife's hand.

She sits down, looking, it has to be said, knock-out in clothes that Slim Keith would maim to wear.

For the first time, she's properly in the room, and the centre of attention. 'First important question,' she demands in that Brigadoon burr of hers. 'Husband, where's my bacon?'

'Ah.' Mr Williams scampers off to the kitchen, leaving me alone with Mrs Williams.

'I'm so sorry. As you'll have gathered, we didn't know that you were coming.' Her candour is refreshing. 'Fact is, it was a late night. It's been a lot of late nights. We must have missed the letter making the appointment. We've been away. Only just got back.'

A signing tour? Reading to children in libraries? Research for (let us pray) a book *not* set in the Cosywolds of Twee Parva on a Saturday afternoon?

'Florida and Washington,' she said. I made sure my eyes did not quite roll. Have things got so bad Tricky Dicky has enlisted the Queen of Fantasy as a special adviser? I don't get to ask my question, as she continues hurriedly. 'Seeing friends and family. They're having a tough time.'

Was she able to help? She looks stricken. 'Really, we just kind of… stood and watched. We don't get involved. Not any more. We do our best. You know – some situations are so unbelievably complex that you can't really…'

There we go, readers. I've offered you a genuine insight. That's why her little books are so simple – it's a counterbalance for the unbearable difficulties of the real world.

'Not that, you know, I don't… in a little way.' Amelia offers me a pained smile. 'Rory and I, well, we have a little money. We do a few things with it. For instance, there was an orphanage…' And suddenly, she's all steel: 'No, I'm not going to tell you where. It was in a terrible state. But, you know, we got involved. We helped out.'

The great thing, by the way, about anonymous acts of charity is that they are Very Hard to check up on to prove that they are real.

As there's nothing more boring than people talking about their Good Causes, I figure we should move on to writing. I ask her where she gets her ideas from, and she gives me A Look. 'What do you want me to say to that?' she laughs. 'What does anyone ever say to that?'

I tell her that some people write about what they know, about their life experiences, about people they've met. I don't know what I'm expecting her to tell me – her books are about magicians, ancient forces, wicked stepmothers and lost children. What can she really know about that sort of thing?

'It's true,' she admits eventually. 'We live a quiet life. We're just living in New York.'

Mr Williams dances back in. He's singing a song about aliens living in New York. He puts a plate of bacon down in front of her and dances back out.

Mrs Williams smiles and leans forward confidentially. A drop of bacon fat pools onto her plate. 'There is a story I want to do… it's about a little girl. She's lost on the streets of New York. She's very lost and she's very alone and she's very frightened.'

'And a good magician turns up and makes her life better?'

She doesn't smile. She just pushes her sandwich from one end of the plate to the other. 'I dunno. I don't think anyone turns up. She just has to make the best of the world on her own.'

'With her magic powers?' I ask. She can't disappoint her readers totally!

She nods. 'With her magic powers... perhaps.' She takes a bite of the sandwich. 'And that's why the late nights. Research. Imagine that – me, a crazy old bag lady wandering the streets of New York looking for a lost girl. But yes, I do go looking for her.'

What, I ask – do you really think the heroine of your book is out there? A little lost girl with magic at her fingertips?

She puts down her sandwich and looks at me. There are tears in her eyes. 'I do.'